St George and the Dragon

LAH.

St George and the Dragon

Beth Andrews

ROBERT HALE · LONDON

ISBN 0 7090 7873 0

Robert Hale Limited
Clerkenwell House
Clerkenwell Green
London EC1R 0HT

2 4 6 8 10 9 7 5 3 1

Typeset in 11½/16pt Sabon
Derek Doyle & Associates, Shaw Heath.
Printed in Great Britain by
St Edmundsbury Press, Bury St Edmunds, Suffolk.
Bound by Woolnough Bookbinding Ltd.

CHAPTER ONE

England, 1816

Sir Lester Malmsbury swung from the chandelier. Having made his ascent by way of a heavy wooden chair perched atop the round table in the centre of the room, he leaped up toward the hanging lamp with its ring of twelve candles, knocking over the chair and sailing high above the other occupants of Miss Honoria Inchwood's salon, most of whom were too castaway to pay any attention to his singular feat.

His flight was brief, his descent spectacular. The ceiling, after all, was not designed to support the weight of a gentleman of some thirteen stone. He glided once to the east and once to the west, before an ominous creak heralded the end of his ride and of the ceiling. The chain gave way, bringing down a rain of wood and plaster, along with Sir Lester, on top of the table – which, in turn, cracked under the onslaught and toppled over, depositing the gentleman on the floor, his fist still clutching the remnants of the chandelier with its extinguished bits of wax and wicks.

There was a short round of applause in appreciation of this acrobatic exhibition.

'Do you think he's dead?' a male voice sounded through the semi-gloom.

'Lay you odds he's not,' another responded.

'Done!'

'Oh Lord!' a feminine voice spoke this time. 'Looks like I'm goin' t' need a new table.'

'Rather more than that, I'd say, Honoria.' The gentleman who responded to her statement was the only man present who did not appear to be completely foxed. Indeed, he was not only quite sober but noticeably unimpressed by the proceedings.

'You're right an' all, Richard,' the lady answered, pushing past a middle-aged gentleman with a half-naked young woman on his lap, neither of whom paid any heed to her presence. 'You don't think he's gone and killed 'imself, do ye?'

Richard bent over the prostrate peer and calmly felt for a pulse. Having ascertained the other man's condition, he straightened and turned to the woman.

'I'm afraid he's still alive, ma'am.'

'Damn!' The gentleman who had wagered against this eventuality was obviously disappointed. 'Are you quite sure, St George?' he asked.

'Perfectly sure,' Richard answered.

'That's one to you, Harry.'

'Told you so.'

Someone lit another lamp, which gave considerably more illumination to the scene. There were several scantily clad ladies twined around a number of intoxicated gentlemen. One or two of the males present had long since drifted into unconsciousness and were lying about on chairs or – in one particular case – under a divan. A few of Miss Inchwood's other clients had already left the main party for some private entertainment in one of her special rooms. Her girls were always ready to oblige any gentleman who had a bit of blunt.

'If you'll excuse me, Honoria,' St George said, surveying his surroundings, 'I'll be on my way.'

'So soon, Richard?' Honoria Inchwood, a faded blonde nearer to forty than thirty, with highly rouged cheeks and wearing an eye-watering orange gown, frowned at him. 'You're not ill, are you?'

'Something of the sort.'

'I'm sure one of my girls would cure whatever ails ye!'

His thin, firm lips barely lifted at the corners. 'Another time, perhaps.'

With a slight bow, he turned and made his exit, grabbing his cloak, hat and cane on his way out. It was past one o'clock in the morning and the streets of London were relatively quiet.

His carriage was waiting at a discreetly correct distance from the entrance to Miss Inchwood's establishment. He did not think he would be returning there any time soon. Somehow, it had lost its charms for him. But then, nothing held much interest for him these days. He was aware of a disquieting feeling of *ennui*, a dissatisfaction with everything and everyone around him.

He must be getting old, he supposed. After all, his fortieth birthday was approaching in a mere two months – early August, in fact. Still, he could not determine any particular reason for his want of spirits. He had recently discarded his last mistress, who had bored him almost as soon as he bedded her. Nor had any of Miss Inchwood's merchandise tempted him tonight. What the devil ailed him?

Within a very few minutes the carriage wheels were rattling to a halt on the cobblestones before his own house in Berkeley Square, a much more fashionable quarter of the city. He descended on to the pavement and prepared to mount the steps, but was halted by the sound of someone hailing him from the other side of the street.

'Hallo, Richard!'

St George had already identified the speaker by his voice, but he turned to see Julian Marchmont striding across the street towards him. Julian was a tall, well-made fellow with golden locks and deep blue eyes. He had only recently achieved his majority and was determined to enjoy it freely and fully.

'Going home so soon?' another voice called out. This was a rather older man: in fact, Julian's uncle, Sir Jasper Marchmont.

'This is no time to be lying abed, Richard,' Julian quizzed him.

'Especially if one is alone. Or is one?' Sir Jasper added, with a knowing look in the general direction of Richard's front door.

'Quite alone.'

'You ain't ill, old boy?' the older man suggested.

'I fear so. And the disease appears to be incurable.'

'Good Lord!' Julian was instantly concerned. 'I had no idea. Why did you not tell me?'

Despite himself, St George laughed. Julian had changed considerably from the green youth who had come to town at the beginning of the season, but he still occasionally displayed a disarming naivete which Richard almost envied. How many years had it been since he would have answered the same?

'I thought it was plain enough,' he said. 'I am sure I display all the most hideous symptoms of chronic boredom.'

Julian shook his head. 'I might have known you were trying to roast me.'

'I?' Richard pretended affront. 'I assure you my condition is pitiable enough.'

'We were just on our way to Miss Inchwood's establishment,'

Henry told him. 'Come with us and see if she can't ease your suffering.'

'I am surprised at you, Marchmont,' Richard chafed him. 'Honoria's house is hardly an appropriate place for you to be taking a babe in arms like your nephew.'

'Gammon!' Julian snorted. 'You've taken me there on more than one occasion yourself. And I am no greenhorn, you know. You are an excellent tutor, sir.'

'Am I?' St George's mouth twisted slightly. 'I wonder if I have taught you anything worth knowing?'

'Can you doubt it?' Julian stared at him in surprise. 'Why, if it had not been for you, I would never have caught that sprig Daniel Afdore, trying to fuzz the cards last week! Saved me quite a bundle, I can tell you.'

'The lad also shows some promise with the foils, from what I hear, and he handles the reins with considerably more skill than was used to be the case. In fact,' his uncle added, 'he is bidding fair to be a notable Corinthian. The pupil may yet outdo his own master.'

'Please!' Richard held up his hand in protest. 'Modesty compels me to beg you to desist from this catalogue of accomplishments, all of which you apparently attribute to my tutelage.'

'Well, sir, will you come with us, then?' Sir Jasper tapped his cane impatiently on the bottom step, where they stood. 'I have no wish to stand here talking all night.'

'Forgive me if I decline the offer. I have, in fact, just come from Miss Inchwood and feel no great temptation to return thither.'

'Then let us come inside with you, Richard,' Julian insisted. 'Perhaps Uncle Jasper and I can help to cheer you up.'

'I have no objection.' St George bowed. 'Though I fear you

are doomed to failure.'

A few minutes later, the trio was ensconced in Richard's sitting-room, each stretched out in a comfortable chair with a glass of wine, which their host's manservant had procured with near-miraculous speed. But it seemed that, rather than lifting the cloud over their friend's head, they were more inclined to become immured in the slough of despond themselves.

'I must confess that the amusements in Town are beginning to lose their appeal,' Julian said.

'Listen to the boy!' his uncle chuckled. 'He talks more like an old man of fifty than a mere lad of one and twenty.'

'He has certainly achieved more notoriety in one season than many men do in a dozen.' St George eyed his young friend with some amusement.

It was perfectly true, however. From the moment Julian appeared in London, he had made a hit. Green he might have been, but he came from a fine old Shropshire family which boasted not merely good breeding but considerable wealth. Such a combination would have guaranteed his social success, but, in addition to all this, he was very good-looking, and though some less charitable members of the *ton* felt that he could have been an inch or two taller, most could find few faults with his person.

Romantic-minded young ladies sighed over him, while their more practical mamas competed vigorously against each other in their attempts to secure his fortune for their daughters. Society matrons proudly displayed him at routs, ridottos and frolics of all kinds; a party was scarcely considered worth attending if it did not boast his presence.

For his part, Julian was eager to cut a dash, which he had certainly managed to do. With his father's blunt, his uncle's connections, and the lessons of Richard St George, he had transformed himself in a matter of weeks from a gawky young colt into a budding Corinthian. His coats were made by Weston, his boots by Hoby, and his golden curls were ruthlessly cut and brushed into a severe Brutus style which was the high kick of fashion for gentlemen.

But as his town bronze increased, his popularity with doting matrons began to decline. Julian made it clear that he was willing enough to flirt with susceptible damsels, but he was more like to trifle with them than to offer for them. Several young ladies were already said to be going into declines after his initial ardour for them had evaporated as quickly as a rain puddle in the sunshine. He was, in fact, gaining a reputation for his dealings with the fair sex. It was not the sort of reputation to which more sober gentlemen aspired. Some high sticklers did not hesitate to declare him a young rake.

But despite his endless round of entertainments, his prize-fights and Paphians, Julian himself was dissatisfied – though he hardly knew why. Perhaps St George's blue devils were proving contagious. After all, if the teacher be cast down, what becomes of his prize pupil?

'I know!' Julian cried out, breaking the dull silence which had descended upon the room. 'A cockfight. The very thing to vanquish devils of any colour – blue, green or violet.'

'What about that pretty ladybird I saw you with last week at Covent Garden, St George?' Sir Jasper asked with a knowing look. 'The little redhead with the breasts like melons? Surely she is enough to gladden any man's heart?'

'When you have known as many women as I have,' Richard told him, 'you'll find that one of them is very much like another. The pleasure they give is scarcely worth the money and time required to keep them.'

'Half the girls in London are mad in love with me,' Julian

complained. 'But what does that matter? Whichever one I choose, I'm well aware that her charms will pall within a fortnight.'

Sir Jasper could not refrain from laughing at this. 'If you are not the two greatest coxcombs I ever encountered. You talk as if you have only to lift your fingers to command the affections of any woman in England!'

'You may laugh,' – Julian sat up in his chair – 'But I don't know any girl in the country I could not have if I set my mind to it. And as for Richard, his reputation with the ladies is the stuff of myth and legend.'

There was another silence, while Sir Jasper examined the two men minutely, his brow furrowed in concentration. Then a singularly wicked smile lifted the corners of his mouth.

'Since you seem so certain of your prowess in the arts of love,' he murmured, 'let me propose a wager, Nephew . . .'

'A wager?' Julian was puzzled. 'What kind of nonsense is this, Uncle?'

'Not nonsense, my boy. I am in deadly earnest.'

For the first time, St George showed a flicker of interest. 'What, precisely, are the terms of this wager, sir?'

Sir Jasper Marchmont leaned back in his chair and folded his hands in an attitude of meditation, tapping the tips of his fingers together as he prepared to speak.

'Well, Uncle?' Julian asked, impatiently.

'Before I state my terms,' the older Marchmont began, 'let me tell you a story.'

'Ah!' St George's eyes narrowed. 'Methinks we are about to be enlightened, Julian.'

Sir Jasper chose to ignore his friend's sarcasm. 'A mile or two from my home in Buckinghamshire – that beautiful county watered by the gently flowing River Ouse – there are the remains of an old Gothic abbey, dating from before good King Henry's time.

'About twelve years ago, one Mr Woodford, a wealthy merchant, bought the property – along with its extensive grounds – and made considerable improvements, although part of the old cloisters are still in a state of ruin. Mr Woodford, perhaps, nourishes a love of the picturesque.'

'I do not see what this has to say to anything, sir,' Julian complained. 'What can the history of Mr Woodford and his folly mean to us?'

'Patience, Nephew. I shall reveal all.' Sir Jasper resumed his tale. 'When Mr Woodford arrived, he brought with him his daughter—'

'Aha!' St George murmured. 'Now we come to it!'

'Please refrain from interrupting me,' Jasper requested tartly, 'or I shall never finish.'

'I beg pardon. Let us return then to the Ouse.'

'He brought with him his daughter,' Sir Jasper repeated, his placidity restored, 'who was then a child of perhaps six or seven years.'

'Which would make her about nineteen at present . . .' Julian ruminated aloud. 'What is she like, Uncle?'

'That,' he replied, 'is for you to discover. And if you do, you will certainly know more than anyone else in the neighbourhood.'

'What do you mean?'

'Mr Woodford,' he explained, 'is a recluse. And his daughter is kept locked and guarded in her Gothic abbey on the edge of the little town of Folbrook, like some enchanted princess in a fairy tale.'

As Henry continued, it transpired that the Woodford family received no visitors to their gloomy abode. Nor did they themselves ever call upon their neighbours. They did not attend church, though it was understood that their household included a private chaplain of considerable age. They had but few servants, considering the size of their estate, and those few were not local people and mingled little with the villagers. When provisions were required, Mr Woodford himself purchased them, or sent his manservant or housekeeper, neither of whom were inclined to be loquacious.

Little was known about what went on up at Folbrook Abbey, and nobody had ever seen Miss Woodford in all the years she had lived there. There were whispers among the country folk. It was said that the poor creature was completely mad, and kept locked in a barred room in the abbey tower.

'Good God!' St George exclaimed. 'Are you quite certain that you have not been reading Mrs Radcliffe again, Jasper? This sounds quite incredible.'

'It is the absolute truth, I assure you. And now,' he said, a faint smirk about his lips, 'the question is, Julian, will you accept my wager?'

'Perhaps I shall – if you would be good enough to tell me precisely what it entails?'

'I will give you, say – one month – to become acquainted with the mysterious Miss Woodford and to use your considerable charm to win her affections.'

Julian paled. 'What!' he cried, staring at his uncle. 'Seduce a woman nobody's ever seen?'

'And one who is scarcely accessible!' St George chuckled. 'Beware, Julian. The abbey may even contain an ogre, which you will have to slay to win the hand of this elusive creature.'

'Not an ogre, St George, but a dragon,' Sir Jasper was eager to inform them. 'She is one Miss Rosalind Powell, an indigent female who is Miss Woodford's constant companion and guardian – a formidable woman in her own right.'

Julian stared. 'It sounds positively medieval, not to mention impossible.'

'You cannot do it, then?' Jasper's smile broadened. 'You refuse the wager?'

Julian looked from Jasper's smiling face to Richard's raised brows. 'Damme,' he said, 'I can't let it be said I refused! For all I know, the girl may be hideously deformed. But though she have three eyes in her head and eight fingers on either hand, I will endeavour to woo her.'

'Let me at least allay your fears on that head,' Sir Jasper assured him. 'I am one of the fortunate few who have seen Miss Woodford – though, to be sure, it was but a brief glimpse.'

A mere three months before, he had been riding from Town at dusk, having been to a blacksmith to have his favourite horse shod. When he encountered a most opulent carriage, he recognized it immediately as belonging to the Woodfords, having once seen it exiting the abbey gates. The blinds were not down and, as he drew abreast of it on the near-deserted stretch of road, he thought to see old Mr Woodford inside. Instead, as he turned his head, he was shocked to see a lovely young woman with golden curls and large blue eyes staring blankly out of the window. He had only a moment to enjoy the view, however, before her companion – almost certainly Miss Powell – reached over and closed the blind with such a vigorous snap that he was sure he heard it even above the pounding of the horses' hooves.

'Is she really a beauty?' Julian enquired.

'A veritable goddess.'

'If you are trying to mislead me—'

'What?' Sir Jasper was reproachful. 'Do you not trust your own uncle, whom you have known since you were in leading strings?'

'Perhaps,' St George suggested, 'that is why he does not trust you.'

'Well,' Julian said, before his uncle could respond to this provocative remark, 'I will accept your wager on one condition.'

'And what is that?'

'That St George here be allowed to accompany me and assist me in my . . . quest.'

Sir Jasper considered the matter. 'I have no objection,' he said at last, 'if St George is willing to lend you his aid.'

'Will you, Richard?' Julian asked him. 'If this Miss Powell is the old harridan my uncle describes, I shall certainly need help in winning her fair charge.'

St George stood. 'As your friend, I can hardly refuse. Besides which, I am undoubtedly intrigued by your uncle's story. It is certainly more entertaining than anything I've heard for many a day.'

'It seems to have cured your megrims,' Julian said, with a smile.

'For the moment.'

'Then it is settled.' Sir Jasper put out his hand. 'The only thing that now remains is to state the terms.'

CHAPTER TWO

'Did Papa deliver a speech?'

'One worthy of Hamlet himself,' Rosalind Powell replied.

'He expects us to succumb to the slings and arrows of outrageous fortune the moment his back is turned, no doubt.'

Rosalind folded her hands and raised her eyes roofward at the memory. 'Dire prognostications fell from his lips at such length, and in such vivid detail, that I can only assume he had recently been reading the book of *Revelation*.'

Miss Cassandra Woodford furrowed her brow. 'Now, my dear Rosalind,' she pronounced, unsuccessfully attempting a deep masculine bass, 'I know that I may rely on your good sense and plain rumgumption! I leave Cassandra to your care. You see to it that my girl comes to no harm, for well I know the dire evils that can befall a helpless female of tender years when she is unprotected and subjected to the tribulations which this world so amply affords—'

This was too much for Rosalind, who succumbed to a fit of giggles, only halting them to protest, 'Really, you should not, Cass! There was never a father who so doted on his daughter, I am very sure.'

'Indeed.' The other girl sighed. 'But in Papa's mind I am a little girl still. I know that when he looks at me, he sees not a young woman of nearly twenty, but a freckled schoolgirl – or, worse yet, an infant scarcely weaned.'

'Uncle Frederick only wants what is best for you.'

'Which is why he insists on confining me to this draughty ruin of a house?' Cassandra suggested, apparently unconvinced.

Rosalind Powell looked about her. They were seated in a large apartment, with a ceiling encrusted with a stucco interpretation of intricate fan vaulting. Rich French tapestries adorned the walls, their vivid colours depicting scenes of chivalric romance. The furniture was heavy and ornate, in keeping with the style of the architecture. But it was quite comfortable and testified to the wealth of its owner, if not his taste, for most of the furnishings had been designed by a fashionable architect and approved by Rosalind herself, Mr Woodford having neither the time nor the inclination for such 'fripperies', as he called them. Mr Woodford's money, however, had not been lavished in vain, and the improvements to the original building were extensive, transforming a crumbling relic into a commodious but pleasing residence which yet managed to retain much of its fascinating antiquity.

Even in winter, Folbrook Abbey's numerous fireplaces kept the chill at bay, and hardly ever sent smoke billowing throughout the house. Now, as spring was about to slip into the warm embrace of summer, it was as pleasant a place as any in England. Except for the line of columns and Gothic arches (original to the building) which adorned the western end of the extensive walled cloisters, there was not much which could, in all conscience, be described as a 'draughty ruin'. The high, vaulted ceiling might be considered cavernous by some who would find it oppressive, perhaps, but Rosalind Powell was too practical and sensible to allow its austere grandeur to overpower her.

'You see yourself as a prisoner, then?' she enquired, pursuing Cassandra's remark.

'Am I not?' Cassandra raised an eyebrow in challenge.

'Perhaps.' Rosalind paused a moment before continuing, 'In which case, I suppose I must be cast in the role of your gaoler, like some dreadful female out of the pages of Richardson?'

'Oh no!' Cassandra's distress was instantaneous. 'Dear, dear Rosalind, forgive me if I seemed to say so. I could never, even for a moment, conceive of anything so dreadful!'

She was almost on the verge of tears, and Rosalind reached forward to take the pale, slender hands she held out. 'Thank you, my dear.' She squeezed the hands, and felt a corresponding pressure. 'Nevertheless, there may be some truth in it. Folbrook Abbey is not a gaol. "Stone walls", as the poet has said, "do not a prison make". But I think your father and I are alike in this: that we see it as a hermitage – a defence, if you will – against the world outside its walls. We neither of us want to see you hurt.'

'You have certainly managed to shut out the world here.'

'I wonder,' Rosalind murmured, 'if that has been wisdom, or folly?'

A frilly white cap appeared round the edge of the large oak door just then, perched atop a smiling, russet-cheeked face.

'Is dinner ready, Ellen?' Rosalind asked, glancing up at the young maid.

'Yes, Miss Rosalind. Cook's just sent me from the kitchen to tell yer you'd better come along before it gets cold.'

'We shall be there directly.' Rosalind schooled herself not to laugh. 'We dare not keep Cook waiting!'

Ellen immediately disappeared and the two girls stood up to make their way arm-in-arm towards the dining-room. This was really a large hall, with a table which could easily seat thirty guests. At one end of this, the two girls sat in solemn state, while the servants brought in a simple meal of mutton and potatoes, with a few side dishes.

'I do miss Papa,' Cassandra admitted, finishing off the last of the food before her. 'It is unusual for him to leave us for such a length of time.'

'Now do not be cast down,' her friend cautioned. 'One month will pass soon enough.'

'It might be as much as six weeks,' Cassandra reminded her. 'We shall certainly be sadly in want of male company.'

'I suppose it is fitting that we reside in an abbey,' Rosalind quizzed her, 'seeing that we live like nuns.'

Cassandra pouted. 'Piety may be all well and good,' she said. 'But, for myself, I would welcome a visit from at least a monk – or two monks, perhaps, since I would undoubtedly monopolize a lone cleric, and would not want you to be excluded from any entertainment.'

'Monks are not generally very entertaining, I believe.'

'Two males, then,' Cassandra amended, 'whatever their vocation in life.'

Rosalind could not resist a smile. 'Even one male visitor here would be unusual; two would have to be regarded as little less than a miracle.'

Three days later, Miss Powell received a letter which spelt an end to the solitude which the ladies of Folbrook Abbey were enduring. Indeed, when Debenham handed it to her, she thought he must have been mistaken, but one glance at the direction disproved this theory. It was certainly addressed to Mr Woodford, and, as he had charged her to open any correspondence which might arrive in his absence, she paused only a moment to examine the exterior.

The large seal bore an imprint which seemed vaguely familiar to her. Rosalind could not deny a strong degree of curiosity as she hastily broke the seal and proceeded to decipher the contents. It required more than one perusal, however, for her 'to comprehend the fantastic tale before her.

'Good God!' she whispered under her breath at one point. 'This must be the ravings of a madman.'

At last she allowed the missive to fall into her lap while she stared at the wall in consternation. A portrait by Gainsborough, depicting a stone-faced lady, luxuriously gowned and coiffed in the style of the previous century, stared back at her.

'What shall I do?' she asked the portrait, but the lady steadfastly refused to respond. What could one expect, however, from such a haughty dame?

Should she acquaint Cassandra with what she had just learned? Was it possible to conceal it from her? And what if it proved to be a cruel hoax of some kind? Nothing remotely resembling this had ever presented itself to her before, and she was sorely tempted to burn the hateful note and to make an attempt at least to put the entire incident from her mind.

A faint tap-tap at the door caused her to turn her head in time to see Cassandra entering behind her.

'My dear, you quite startled me!' she exclaimed.

'Am I intruding?' Cassandra halted just inside the door.

'Not at all.'

'I heard that the mail had arrived.' She came forward, passing her hand along the arm of the chair opposite to Rosalind, and sat down. 'More tradesmen's bills, I suppose?'

'Not exactly.'

Cassandra's ears were ever sharp. She must have caught the hesitation in Rosalind's voice, for she cocked her head knowingly, and demanded, 'What is it, Lindy?'

Now was the moment for her to dismiss the matter and set Cassandra's mind at ease. It would take only a word or two: a harmless subterfuge, which was all for the best.

'I have received a letter for your father which purports to be from our neighbour, Sir Jasper Marchmont.'

'Sir Jasper! What reason could he have for writing to us?' Rosalind could not blame the other girl for her surprise. The surrounding families had long since abandoned any efforts to seek social intercourse with the Woodfords when it became obvious that even the kindest of invitations would be refused. The more top-lofty ones had never been more than mildly curious, in any case. For them to receive a letter from any of their neighbours was quite unprecedented.

'He is not reticent in the matter of explanations for his behaviour,' Rosalind said.

'I am absolutely eaten up with curiosity!' Cassandra leaned forward eagerly. 'Pray read the letter to me.'

Having gone this far, Rosalind could hardly refuse her request now. She still did not know why she had not remained silent, but somehow she did not like the thought of deceiving Cassandra.

'*Dear Sir,*' she began, noting, 'It is dated three days ago.'

'Yes, yes.' Cassandra was growing impatient. 'Do go on.'

' "*Please forgive my boldness in thus addressing you, a comparative stranger. I do not doubt that you will understand my importunity when you have heard what I am constrained to relate to you in the strictest confidence. Certain information has come to my attention which necessitates a disclosure of the most painful and distressing nature, involving as it does my own flesh and blood—*" '

'What can he mean?'

'Allow me to continue, my dear Cass, and you shall learn.'

'Forgive me. But indeed, it sounds so fantastic.'

'Oh, the best is yet to come.'

Rosalind continued to read, attempting to keep her voice as cool and composed as possible. It was not easy, considering the nature of the words before her. Sir Jasper related the essential details of the wager which St George and Julian had made, leaving out only the name of the person who had suggested so repulsive a scheme.

'I can hardly believe it!' Cassandra's face was a study in perplexity and total surprise.

'If what our correspondent says is true,' Rosalind said, reasonably, 'it will not be long before it is proved. We have only to wait for the arrival of the two gentlemen in question.'

'But you had not yet finished the letter,' the other girl reminded her.

'There is not much more to relate,' Rosalind confessed. 'He expresses his concern for your welfare – and my own, since it seems that this Julian's confederate has the task of distracting my attention – and apologizes on his nephew's behalf, and then concludes: "*I only hope that, by acquainting you with these particulars, and trusting to your discretion, I will have managed to avert any damage to the reputation of your fair daughter, and that there will be no further distress caused by my nephew's scandalous behaviour . . . I remain, sir, Your Humble Svt., etc., etc.*" '

'Well, this is certainly more entertaining than a receipt from the blacksmith's!'

'I am glad that you are taking it in such a charitable spirit.' Rosalind could not repress a sigh of relief. 'I was afraid that it might oppress you somewhat.'

'Oppress me!' Cassandra's laugh was gay and strong. 'How could you think so? Why, this is the most wonderful news!'

'I would not place it in quite so kindly a light.'

'I have heard Papa say several times that Julian Marchmont is a buck of the first head. I can hardly wait to meet him.'

'Meet him?' Rosalind almost jumped from her chair. 'There is no chance of that happening – not as long as I have anything to say about it.'

'You cannot be so chicken-hearted, Lindy,' the younger girl complained.

'I? Chicken-hearted?' Miss Powell was conscious of a feeling of acute annoyance at this slur upon her courage.

'Well, I think you are,' Cassandra told her. 'You seem quite afraid of meeting the two gentlemen.'

Her annoyance grew. 'Two rakes, may I remind you,' she said, scowling.

'Well, that is better than two monks.' Cassandra smiled her loveliest smile – one of pure delight. 'It was you who complained that monks were rather dull company – which I'll wager rakes are not likely to be.'

'No indeed.'

'Imagine being courted by such a man.'

'Imagine being seduced and ruined by one.'

Cassandra shrugged. 'But since we are already forewarned—' she began.

'In this case, that is small consolation.' Rosalind stood and began pacing about the room in some agitation. 'For heaven's sake, Cass, only think how foolish it would be to encourage the attentions of such men! We are totally unskilled in arts of which they are undoubtedly masters.'

'So you *are* afraid of them,' Cassandra quizzed.

'No.' She halted before the younger girl. 'I am merely being prudent.'

'I understand that Julian is excessively handsome,' Cassandra murmured dreamily. 'All the young ladies in London are positively enraptured by him.'

'As I am never likely to meet him, that can be of no interest to me,' Rosalind insisted.

'Well, a handsome face is not likely to turn *my* head.'

'No.' Rosalind swallowed something in her throat. 'That is one eventuality I need not fear, at least. Still, I cannot but wish them as far away from here as may be possible.'

'In Timbuktu, perhaps?'

'If wishes were horses,' Rosalind admitted, 'they should certainly be galloping somewhere in the vicinity of North Africa at this moment.'

'You are perfectly right, of course.' Cassandra sighed. 'We should have nothing to do with them.'

'I am glad to hear you say so.' Rosalind looked down upon that innocent face, with its strange, faraway expression. 'But we need not worry. They will not find it so easy to make our acquaintance. This is one hen house those two foxes will not enter with impunity.'

CHAPTER THREE

'I loathe the country!' Julian scraped the toe of his boot savagely against the gnarled trunk of an ancient oak, in an unsuccessful attempt to remove the cow pats in which he had so recently trod. 'I was happy enough to quit it and escape to London.'

'Then you should be happy to be here.' Richard yawned. 'You will appreciate the pleasures of Town all the more upon your return from this delightful hamlet.'

'Damn my uncle! I must have been mad to agree to anything so idiotic.'

'Such ingratitude, my boy!' Richard shook his head in mock censorship. 'I, on the other hand, am revelling in the rustic joys of our little holiday. It brings out the poet in me. I am of a mind to write a sonnet, or at least a lyrical quatrain:

> *To trip through meadows green and sweet,*
> *And breathe the fragrant air so pure;*
> *To wander in such calm retreat . . .*'

'And frolic in the cow manure!' Julian finished his flight of fancy with more relish than polish.

'Please remember,' Richard prodded, 'that a thousand

pounds hangs in the balance – not to mention your reputation, my lad.'

Julian propped himself up against the oak tree while his companion rested on a crumbling stone wall. They were at the edge of a large field of grain, and might have been the only two inhabitants of the surrounding area, for there was no other sign of human life, but for the thatched roof of a small cottage peeping up from behind a thick coppice at the opposite side.

'This is far more difficult than I had imagined,' Julian confessed, with a decided pout.

'We were not exactly ignorant of the difficulty,' St George reminded him. 'If it were too easy, your uncle would have been a fool to make such a wager – which, alas, he is not. Besides, what would be the challenge in a prize which required no effort to gain?'

'But it is impossible.'

Julian's words, though despondent, certainly seemed to state the present case with accuracy. They had been in Buckinghamshire for five days, and had so far been denied even the smallest glimpse of their too elusive quarry. Their cards had been presented at Folbrook Abbey, but their attempts to gain admittance had been firmly – and none too politely – rebuffed. Neither gentleman was accustomed to such treatment, but St George was inclined to take the matter more philosophically than his young friend.

'By all ordinary means,' he said now, 'it would certainly appear to be impossible. But when ordinary means fail, one is then forced to attempt the extraordinary.'

'What do you mean?'

Richard folded his hands together, gazing up at the heavens as if in prayer, his eyes not quite closed but definitely narrowed – though this was caused not by religious fervour but by the brightness of the early afternoon sun, which necessitated a slight squint.

'I see that you still have much to learn, young man.' He did not look at Julian, but did not need to do so. He could well imagine the shade of annoyance which passed over the other man's countenance. 'Though the fox may hide, the hounds will scour the countryside until they have cornered him in his lair. Resourcefulness and determination may yet win the day.'

'Does this fine speech indicate that you have a plan?'

'Now do not be impertinent when addressing your master,' Richard warned him. 'You insisted on my presence here, after all. And you undoubtedly need my considerable experience, since it appears that you are unable to find a solution to your present dilemma on your own.'

'Pray enlighten me, then, my noble oracle.'

'What say you to a little – how shall I put it? – exploration?'

'Exploration!'

'After all, we had planned to have some pigeon fricassee this evening for dinner. But the two particular birds we are seeking are kept in a decidedly remote dovecote.' St George cocked his head in the general direction of the abbey. 'We have walked this far out of sheer boredom. Over that hillock, less than two miles hence, lies our destination – perhaps even our destiny. And even the most well-guarded birdcage must have a door some-where . . . .'

'Or perhaps a window.' A faint smile began to draw the corners of Julian's mouth upwards. 'Let us waste no more time, then. Once more into the breach!'

An hour later, he was not so sanguine. They had trudged the rocky country lanes and waded through grassy meadows, working themselves into a fine, manly sweat. Having at last reached the abbey, however, their task seemed more daunting than ever. It was set in the centre of a large park, through which they certainly should not have been wandering. And the whole of the main building was surrounded by a wall which an Alpine goat would have found difficult to scale.

'We might as well return home,' Julian said, in disgust, as they carefully edged their way along the perimeter. 'Even could we surmount this cursed wall, there are no doubt hounds on the other side which would likely tear us to pieces in a minute.'

'Or perhaps,' St George suggested, 'the master of the house would have us dragged off into a dungeon – an oubliette, I fancy – where we should be tortured and starved to death, our bones being discovered a few centuries hence, chained to the wall.'

'The master of the house is away,' Julian reminded him, impervious to sarcasm. 'That is about the only thing we have so far learned in our favour.'

'I may be at ease, then.'

'I am happy that you find the situation so amusing.'

'I am deriving a certain amount of perverse pleasure from your plight, I must admit.'

'I wish that I could perceive the humour in losing a thousand pounds. But at present I must— Hallo!'

This soft exclamation escaped from Julian's lips as he halted at the edge of a large wooden door which was set into the wall. It was surrounded by thick vines, so that one would not perceive it until standing directly before it. But though the vegetation might be heavy, it was well pruned, so it seemed that the door might be used by the occupants of the abbey upon occasion, and was not permanently sealed.

'Aha!' Richard chuckled. 'Heaven has heard our prayers.'

Julian scratched his chin, surveying the wooden impediment.

'Do you think we might be able to pick the lock?'

'Alas,' St George said with an exaggerated sigh. 'Though I know it must sink me in your estimation, I confess that picking locks is an accomplishment I have never mastered. For some reason or other, the opportunity never came much in my way.'

'I do not think we could break it down. It looks quite solid.'

'I do not intend to make the attempt. Besides,' he added reasonably, 'it would be bound to attract a great deal of attention. Battering through wood is a rather noisy business.'

'True.' Julian's countenance fell once more. 'Do you think I might try to climb up the ivy? Would it support my weight?'

'Possibly.' St George considered the matter. 'But we might try other means . . . .'

With that, he brushed past his friend, leaned forward and twisted the heavy iron handle on the door. With the faintest click, it swung open, revealing a large open area of neatly planted herbs and flowers and a courtyard with a small fountain bubbling at its centre. There were arched colonnades on three sides and a statue of the Madonna and child gracing the central arch at the back.

'Well.' Julian sounded slightly disappointed. 'I certainly never expected so easy an entrance. I am almost inclined to believe that you had it all arranged, sir.'

'I have neither such foresight, nor such influence,' Richard said, closing the door behind him. 'But although it has prevented me from enjoying the spectacle of watching you attempt to scale the wall, I am grateful for the negligence of whichever servant forgot to lock it.'

He had scarcely finished speaking when there was an ominous growl from somewhere close by.

'The hounds!' Julian hissed, looking about him with some

apprehension. 'Said I not so?'

'So you did,' Richard admitted. 'But it is even worse than you imagined, for this particular hound seems to add invisibility to his other demonic attributes.'

They certainly saw nothing beyond the low hedge a few feet to the left of them, from which the growls continued to issue.

'He must be crouched behind it,' Julian said, backing toward the closed door, in preparation for a quick retreat, should the beast spring out upon them.

'Welly!' a soft voice called, from the shadows of the colonnade. 'What is it, boy?'

Both men looked toward the spot from whence the sound had issued. But whoever the lady might be, she was concealed by the row of columns.

'Welly!' the hidden female called again, more firmly. 'Come here, boy!'

At this, there was a furious rustling beyond the hedge, before a small, dark-haired ball of fur dashed into the middle of the pathway on which they stood. Planting his four paws squarely on the stones, he proceeded to address them in a burst of nasal, high-pitched barking.

'A pug!'

The disgust in Julian's tone was too much for St George, who began to chuckle. This was the most deliciously absurd scene!

'Welly!' the lady called for the third time. 'What is wrong? Is someone there?'

'What are we to do now?' Julian whispered urgently to his friend.

'Screw your courage to the sticking place, lad,' Richard advised. 'You are a timid hunter, to be sure.'

'Well, if it comes to that—'

'Hush!' Richard interrupted his outburst. 'We have our

quarry in sight. One false move may ruin all.'

'Oh.' Julian looked decidedly confused.

'I pray you,' Richard called out loudly, 'call off this ferocious animal, ma'am! We are not housebreakers. I assure you that we mean no harm.'

There was a moment of silence, before the elusive lady spoke once more to the dog, this time very sharply, insisting that he come to her *at once*. Apparently, the redoubtable Welly at last recognized the voice of authority. With one final, defiant 'woof!', he turned and scampered off into the courtyard toward his mistress.

'You are perfectly safe now, gentlemen,' she sang out, a moment later.

'I think she means for us to approach,' Richard suggested, since Julian hesitated.

With a lowering glance at his partner, he moved forward. In less than a minute, they had traversed the distance to the centre of the courtyard, and turned to face the row of gothic arches from whence the lady's voice had come. As they did so, a slim figure rose from a stone bench placed against the inner wall and came slowly towards them out of the shadows, the pug known as 'Welly' still growling behind her skirts.

As she stepped into the sunlight, Richard was not surprised to hear Julian catch his breath. She was one of the loveliest creatures he himself had ever beheld in a life filled with many pretty ladybirds. She was like a porcelain figurine come to life, in a pink-and-white muslin dress, with a pink-and-white complexion to match, and divinely blue eyes which seemed to look through rather than at them. Her voice, which they had already heard, was low-toned and pleasing, and her smile – which they now beheld for the first time – was brighter than the sunshine, with small, even white teeth glistening between deliciously curved lips.

Had he been a younger man, Richard reflected, he might well have experienced something more than mere admiration. As it was, he acknowledged her undoubted charms and wished Julian every success. She was an English rose, waiting to be plucked.

'Permit me to introduce myself, ma'am.' Julian now hastened to attract the lady's attention. 'Julian Marchmont at your service.'

She turned her head towards him, but was prevented from commenting by Richard's own tardy introduction. She did not acknowledge their bows, but stood there with her head slightly tilted to one side, as though considering the situation.

'I,' she said at length, 'am Cassandra Woodford. Forgive me if I neglect my manners, but it is not often that I confront two strange men in my garden.'

'We called here several days ago and presented our cards.' Julian sounded aggrieved.

'We never receive visitors, I'm afraid.'

'Why not, Miss Woodford?' Richard enquired.

'It is my father's wish.'

'Forgive me for saying, that seems even more gothick than our present surroundings.'

She laughed: a curiously gay, carefree sound in the solemn stillness.

'Are our surroundings so terribly gloomy?' she asked.

'You do not find them so?' Julian looked about him at the high stone walls, adding, 'But perhaps you have become accustomed to it all.'

'It is not unattractive,' Richard interjected. 'But one must admit that it could hardly be referred to as "cheerful". Would you not agree, Miss Woodford?'

'As to that, sir,' the young lady replied, 'you would do better to seek Rosalind's opinion.'

'Rosalind?' Richard was pleased to find her so free with her information.

'Rosalind Powell,' she elucidated. 'She is my companion, though much more like an older sister to me. She helped my father oversee the reconstruction of the abbey before we moved here from Yorkshire. Most of the interior furnishings were chosen by her.'

'She might be well qualified to pass judgement,' Julian said persuasively, 'but you surely must have some views on the subject. It is your home.'

'True,' she acknowledged. 'But in such matters I confess that I do rely on Rosalind's opinions. She is much more familiar with Folbrook Abbey than I am. I have never actually seen it, after all.'

'Never seen it?' Julian's exclamation echoed Richard's own surprise. He looked intently into the bright, inscrutable blue eyes of the goddess before them, holding his breath for a moment as he waited for her to respond.

'No.' She seemed to stare into the distance, at some invisible point between them. 'You see, I am blind.'

CHAPTER FOUR

St George had no doubt of Miss Woodford's sincerity. The wonder was that he had not realized before. Poor Julian looked as though he had just seen a ghost. The truth was, they were so preoccupied with the lady's beauty that they had failed to notice anything else unusual about her. Now it was painfully plain, and pity mingled with a kind of nervous embarrassment at the unexpected turn which their interview had taken.

What either would have said in response to her statement, they would never know. As they stood there in the sunshine, a strange hissing sound broke the sudden stillness. Almost simultaneously, a thin dark object streaked out of the sky to land with a thump on the grassy space between the stones at Richard's feet.

'Good God!' Julian exclaimed, staring at the ground before his friend.

Richard's gaze also lowered, but he made no comment as he surveyed the object – an arrow – its head buried in the earth where it had fallen less than twelve inches from the toes of his boots.

'You would not happen to have any savage Indians from the wilds of America residing here, Miss Woodford?' he asked, bending to retrieve the arrow.

'Or a descendant of William Tell, perhaps?' Julian suggested.

'Oh dear!' Miss Woodford put up a delicate hand to cover her lips. 'That must have been Rosalind.'

'Miss Powell has a most unusual way of greeting guests,' Richard commented. 'A few inches nearer and I would have become the new "Ghost of Folbrook Abbey".'

Cassandra laughed outright.

'Then,' Julian added, 'we might have asked, "Who killed Cock Robin?".'

' "I, said the Sparrow – with my bow and arrow",' a voice answered from the shadowed colonnade. ' "I killed Cock Robin".'

A moment later, the elusive Diana appeared. She was no sparrow, however, Richard considered: more like a peacock. Rosalind Powell was somewhat shorter than Miss Woodford, and, where Cassandra was divinely fair, her companion was possessed of lustrous dark hair and eyes to match. She had her own exotic beauty, more like a gypsy than a proper Englishwoman. She appeared to be about five-and-twenty, though that might be deceptive.

'My compliments, ma'am.' St George bowed to her. 'A fine shot, indeed.'

'But a little short of the target,' she replied. Her eyes sparked with fire and she moved to link her arm with Cassandra's, as though to protect her from them. A dragon indeed!

'Nonsense!' Cassandra seemed to find it even more amusing. 'Papa says Lindy's aim is deadly accurate. I'm quite sure that she never meant to harm you. She would not put an arrow through a visitor. At least, I do not think she would.'

'I have no desire to contradict either you or your esteemed father,' St George said smoothly. 'And I am grateful for Miss Powell's restraint.'

'And may I ask,' the redoubtable Miss Powell interrupted, 'what you two are doing here?'

'We were exploring the countryside, and happened upon this most interesting building.'

'To which you gained access without permission,' she shot back. 'How did you get in here?'

' "With love's light wings did I o'erperch these walls",' Julian said, dramatically.

'That is from *Romeo and Juliet*.' Cassandra Woodford correctly identified the quotation.

'Then let me reply with something from *Macbeth*,' Rosalind was quick to respond. ' "Stand not upon the order of your going, but go at once".'

'Do not be rude to our guests, dear Lindy,' Cassandra chastized gently.

'Guests!' Rosalind arched delicate eyebrows. 'Did you invite them, then? – for I am very sure that *I* did not. And if love brought them hither, it must have been self-love – and it had better bear them hence just as lightly.'

'No,' the younger girl confessed, 'I did not invite them, but they are here now and possibly tired from their long walk. Perhaps they would like some refreshment.'

'Shall I fetch a pail of water, then?'

'Your hospitality, Miss Woodford, is much appreciated.'

Richard ignored the last remark from Miss Powell. 'But we do not wish to intrude where we are not welcome.'

'Very wise of you,' the dragon snapped.

'Rosalind, remember that these gentlemen are strangers here.' Cassandra smiled once more. 'As Christians, it is our duty to treat them with kindness.'

'My dear Miss Woodford, you are all goodness.' Julian stepped forward, at which the little pug growled once more.

'Nor do I blame your companions for guarding you so fiercely. It is rather to their credit.'

With that, he knelt down and called to Welly to come to him. The little dog hesitated for a moment; then, quite unexpectedly, he trotted forward and sniffed Julian's outstretched hand before sitting quietly and allowing the man to stroke his head.

'Well,' Richard commented, smiling, 'at least one of your companions is not as ferocious as first appears.'

'Has he made friends with Welly?' Cassandra enquired, apparently very pleased. 'You are honoured, sir. There are not many people whom he favours.'

'I am indeed fortunate, then.'

'I trust,' Cassandra offered, a little diffidently, 'that you have not been too offended by your reception today.'

'Not at all,' Richard assured her. 'Our introduction might have been unorthodox but it was most entertaining.'

'Then you would not be averse to joining us for supper – perhaps tomorrow evening?'

'Cassandra!' Rosalind Powell was clearly shocked.

'Despite Miss Powell's disapproval,' St George quipped, 'I think I speak for us both when I say that we would be delighted to accept your invitation.'

'How could you do something so foolhardy, Cass!' Rosalind cried, as soon as the two men made their exit the same way they had entered. She followed them to the garden door and made very sure that it was securely locked behind them.

'I am having such fun, Lindy!' the other girl answered, eyes and cheeks aglow. 'You must not spoil it for me now.'

'You know their purpose in coming here,' her companion reminded her.

'What do they look like?' Cassandra asked, ignoring this

unnecessary comment.

'What matter is it how they look?'

'Well, if they are rakes,' she reasoned, 'they must be at least passably good-looking.'

Rosalind hesitated, dwelling on the recent encounter. Her mind's eye pictured precisely how the two men had looked. Julian Marchmont was well proportioned with hair almost as fair as Cassandra's, though his eyes were brown rather than the expected blue which usually accompanies such a complexion. Richard St George, however, was another matter. A few inches taller than his friend, he had the bearing of an athlete, with broad shoulders and lean hips. His brown hair was styled *à la Brutus* and his attire was of a severe but exquisite cut which no provincial tailor had produced. Weston, probably. But it was his eyes which she remembered best. Pure hazel, there was a mocking gleam in them which she found extremely irritating.

'They are both remarkably handsome,' she replied honestly to Cassandra's question, though it cost her something to admit it.

'How thrilling to be pursued by two such men! Do you not think so, Lindy?'

'I feel like a fox being chased by two snarling hounds.' Rosalind opened the door leading from the cloisters into a large, airy hall. 'Such thrills I would gladly relinquish to some other unfortunate female.'

'Mr Marchmont has a lovely voice,' Cassandra said dreamily. 'Manly, to be sure, but strangely warm and gentle. I can tell much from a person's voice, and I know that he has a kind heart.'

'No doubt he is a paragon of masculine virtue,' Rosalind concurred with feigned sweetness. 'Of course, one must over-look his occasional seduction of innocent virgins. Eccentric, perhaps, but wealthy young men must have their diversions.'

'You are determined to dislike them,' the younger girl chided.

'That,' Rosalind said, 'requires no determination on my part at all: merely a knowledge of their character.'

'Well, Providence has placed them in our path.' Cassandra raised her chin in a gesture with which Rosalind was quite familiar. 'And since such a romantic adventure is unlikely to come our way again, I intend to enjoy the situation thoroughly.'

'Are you at all aware of the danger to you – to us both?'

Those blank blue eyes seemed alight with mischief.

'My dear Lindy, that is what makes it all so exciting!'

'I fear I cannot be so sanguine about it.' Rosalind sighed. 'The die is cast, however. We cannot withdraw your invitation – unless I were to send them a note claiming that you were suddenly taken ill.'

'Then you would be telling a lie – which is hardly the Christian thing to do, is it?'

'In this instance, I think my Maker would pardon a little subterfuge.'

'But I would not.'

They had reached the end of the hall and entered a more intimate sitting-room where they made their way to a small settee and seated themselves. Rosalind looked again at the beautiful young girl beside her. She seemed more alive then ever. The advent of those two horrible men seemed to act on her like a tonic.

'You know, Cass,' Miss Powell observed, watching her keenly, 'it is very strange that Debenham should have left that door into the cloisters unlocked.'

'Yes indeed.' Pale-pink lips were caught between pearly white teeth. 'He is always so careful.'

'Unless, of course, he was instructed to leave it unlocked.'

There was a moment of silence, broken by a sudden burst of youthful laughter.

'Dear Lindy.' Cassandra could barely contain her mirth. 'You know me too well.'

'You were never one to brook any opposition when you wanted something.'

'And I fully intended to meet the two gentlemen, whatever you might say,' she admitted without a trace of remorse. 'Now do not fret. We are embarking on the most wonderful adventure of our lives. Someday you will see that I am right about this.'

The battle was lost. The enemy had been allowed – even encouraged – to enter their sanctuary, much as the Trojans gleefully pulled the great horse through their city gates and so sealed their own fate. Miss Woodford, however, while she might bear the name of a prophetess of doom, seemed blissfully unaware of any imminent disaster. She did not even have the excuse of ignorance, for she was well aware of the trap into which she stepped so blithely.

'It seems,' Rosalind muttered to her reflection in the mirror on the wall of her bedchamber, 'that I alone am left to defend the citadel.'

Her enemies, she grudgingly admitted, were formidable. In spite of her knowledge of their intent, and having nerved herself to despise them, she found that she could not deny their undoubted charm. As for their looks, at least Cassandra had the advantage there. But still, she was young and innocent; she knew little of the ways of the world. Come to that, what did *she* – what did Miss Rosalind Powell – know? Rosalind had been sent by her family to live with her uncle and to be a companion to his daughter when she was not yet thirteen years of age. She was now just shy of thirty, and had led a life almost as sheltered as that of her cousin.

She knew nothing of rakes or of the world outside these walls, except for what she had read in books. Nevertheless, that reading had been extensive, as her uncle allowed her complete freedom in the choice of books from his library. He himself rarely read anything but the papers from London and the works of Shakespeare, which had given him an unfortunate penchant for dramatic utterances of considerable length.

She felt that she had acquitted herself quite well in their skirmish this afternoon. Tomorrow night was another matter. She must consider carefully what action to take. She must formulate her battle plan with care. Experience she might lack, but not courage.

Even so, she would have given a great deal to know just what the two gentlemen in question were thinking at this moment.

CHAPTER FIVE

'It is too horrible. I cannot do it.'

Trudging back toward his uncle's house, Julian Marchmont was as vehement in his sudden repudiation of their schemes as he had previously been eager to implement them.

'My dear Julian,' St George counselled, 'do not allow yourself to be overset by what we have discovered today.'

'Overset!' Julian kicked at a stone along the rough path and sent it rolling into the grass. 'She is blind, Richard. How can I even contemplate something so – so obscene?'

'You find it acceptable to seduce a young girl with sight, but not one without.' St George rubbed his chin thoughtfully. 'That is a distinctly odd sort of morality, I would say.'

Julian was not pleased with this ruthless logic.

'It *seems* worse, somehow.'

'It merely means,' his friend said reasonably, 'that you cannot depend upon your good looks to ingratiate yourself with the lady, my young popinjay.'

'I am ready to abandon the scheme altogether.'

'For the lady's sake, or for your own?'

'What do you mean?' Julian demanded.

'Do you fear that, without the aid of your physical appearance, you are incapable of winning your uncle's wager?'

Julian frowned. 'You must admit that it considerably lessens my chances of success.'

St George, however, would not allow this to be the case. He urged the younger man to consider their situation. The two ladies were young, lovely and apparently sheltered from the world. Miss Woodford was obviously already interested and eager to further their acquaintance. It would be odd indeed if she did not respond to masculine charm and flattery.

'And Miss Powell?' Julian asked drily.

'Miss Powell is clearly not a fool. She is highly suspicious of us and of our intentions.'

'If that be the case, she will block us at every turn,' Julian protested. 'How can we hope to succeed?'

'Leave Miss Powell to me,' Richard answered. 'She is a stubborn and independent filly, but she can be . . . mounted.'

'You are a heartless devil, Richard.' Julian looked at his friend as though seeing him for the first time.

St George shrugged. 'Hearts are fine organs for circulating the blood, my idealistic friend. But where women are concerned, a man had better not be guided by them. Use your wits, rather than your feelings, and all will be well.'

Later, at the hunting lodge, St George sat alone, contemplating the events of the day. Sir Jasper had certainly set them a hard task, but he'd swear it was one well worth the effort. In spite of his words to Julian, he still was not certain that they would succeed.

Miss Woodford was undoubtedly a diamond of the first water. Her one defect did not detract from her beauty. Indeed, it might prove to be a boon to them. She had obviously been well guarded by her father and the redoubtable Miss Powell, and he'd wager that she knew nothing of men or their relations with the weaker sex. It could well be easier than Julian imagined to engage her interest and accomplish her seduction.

The beautiful dragon was another matter. She was far younger and much more beautiful than Richard had anticipated, and there was no denying that she was intrepid enough to tackle any man. He could not suppose, however, that Mr Woodford would have engaged her as his daughter's companion had her reputation not been irreproachable. But while her tongue might be as sharp as the arrows she did not hesitate to dispatch at unwelcome visitors, he fancied that she was every bit as unaccustomed to the attentions of gentlemen as Miss Woodford.

He had to confess to himself that he found her fascinating and looked forward to her conquest with greater pleasure than he had felt for anything in some time. He did not usually trifle with the infantry, finding younger women shallow, silly and too easy prey for his talents. But this was no ordinary young lady. No, this was a challenge which roused all his sporting instincts.

He must carefully consider his tactics. She was not likely to be won by ordinary means. She had already shown that she was more than a match for any man whose methods were too obvious and brash. No. He must study her better. Her eyes might blaze with anger and defiance, but that only showed that she was capable of strong emotion – always a weakness, as far as he was concerned. He had only to discover the chink in her armour and pry away the hard shell which protected her heart to uncover the softness beneath it. Once he possessed her, of course, her charms would fade – as did all women's.

In the meantime, he would enjoy the chase, and gladly leave her young charge to his friend's tender mercies.

As for Julian Marchmont, his sleep that night was disturbed by thoughts which were far from pleasant. He had begun this enterprise with a light heart and a conscience untroubled by pangs of guilt or shame. After meeting Miss Woodford, though, he began to feel the first sharp pricking at his heart, which was not nearly as light as it had been formerly.

Miss Cassandra Woodford was like a fairy-tale princess. She possessed a beauty as divine as it was fragile. It even seemed that she was under a strange enchantment which had taken away her sight, so that she was incapable of seeing the evils of the world around her and the deceptiveness of men. Locked in her ancient castle, guarded by an attendant sorceress who dispensed magic arrows at those who dared to encroach upon their domain, she seemed to be waiting to be rescued by a handsome prince.

Alas, Julian reflected, staring up at the ceiling, he was no prince. He was come not to rescue but to rob her of her tranquillity as well as her virginity. He was the lowest worm that ever crawled the earth!

Yet he had made the wager, and his uncle would only laugh if he could know the scruples which suddenly distressed him. Richard certainly found his doubts absurd. After all, he could not, in honour, draw back from the wager. What a poltroon he would look! Yet he could see no glory or honour in the course to which he had committed himself.

With a muttered curse, he closed his eyes and attempted to banish his doubts. He had gone too far to allow remorse to check him now. Yet it was beginning to dawn upon him that he might well derive greater pleasure from losing this particular wager than he ever could from winning it.

CHAPTER SIX

The following day was one of great bustle and excitement at Folbrook Abbey. Though Miss Powell might not relish the evening ahead, she was too well bred to allow the two gentlemen into the house without ensuring that all was in order.

'Sure, 'tis a miracle!' Ellen remarked to her in wonder.

'I am well aware that my uncle would strongly disapprove of this invitation.' Rosalind shook her head, silently chiding herself for submitting so easily to Cassandra's whims.

' 'Tis best the master's not here,' Ellen admitted. 'But if you ask me, ma'am, it's about time both you and Miss Cassandra had some gentlemen callers!'

'To what purpose?' Rosalind asked, not without an edge of irony. 'It is highly unlikely that either of us will ever marry. Cassy's blindness and my lack of fortune are liabilities which few eligible men are likely to overlook.'

'Depends on the gentleman.' Ellen gave her a saucy grin. 'You both have enough assets to tempt any man with eyes in his head.'

'To tempt them – yes, perhaps,' Rosalind agreed, without any false modesty. 'But not, I fear, to marriage.'

The maid laughed out loud at this, and urged Miss Powell not to be saying things to throw her into whoops. Rosalind obliged, and went upstairs to find Cassandra.

Cassandra's maid, Harriet, was busy arranging her golden curls *a là Grecque*. She was positively glowing with anticipation, smiling and laughing up at Rosalind as she heard her enter the bedchamber.

'What time is it, Lindy?' Her ringlets bobbed as she turned about on her seat.

'Half past six,' Rosalind answered. 'It will be another hour before the wolves enter our fold.'

'But they will find that we are not the innocent lambs they take us for,' Cass reminded her.

'I still believe this to be madness.'

'You speak like an old woman,' her young friend quizzed her.

'Old women generally have much more sense than young ones.'

'But rarely do they have an adventure like this one!'

There was no denying the truth of her last remark, so Rosalind contented herself with a brief rehearsal of her plans for the evening. She must keep her wits about her if she would match them against two such opponents. It was obvious that Cassandra intended to derive as much pleasure as possible from their situation. And why not? Her youth was slipping quietly away, and who could tell whether such a chance would come her way again? Madness or not, she was human enough to want more from life than placid propriety.

Cassandra rehearsed their schemes with great enthusiasm, her anticipation growing every minute.

'What fun we shall have!' she exclaimed, looking more animated than Rosalind had seen her in a long time. 'I can hardly wait until supper.'

'I had better go and get dressed myself,' she said at last, rising from her seat on the side of Cassandra's bed.

'Harriet will assist you,' Cass told her. 'And, for Heaven's sake, Lindy,' she added, 'do not wear one of your dowdy governess-looking gowns.'

'I shall find something appropriate, I am sure.'

Cassandra groaned. 'I can just imagine what it will look like. Actually,' she amended, 'I cannot. But Ellen will tell me all.'

'Well,' Rosalind said, trying to bring her high flight down to earth again, 'I cannot be expected to outshine the daughter of the house, can I?'

'I have it on excellent authority that you are a beauty,' the younger girl warned. 'So do not attempt to bamboozle me. You shall wear something pretty and festive and we shall both dazzle our visitors.'

'If I wore sackcloth and ashes, no doubt they would confess themselves enraptured by my beauty.'

'But you shall wear nothing of the kind.' Cassandra returned to the maid. 'Harriet, I charge you to make sure that Miss Rosalind is quite ravishing. I will not be satisfied with less, do you understand?'

'Yes, miss.' Harriet smiled. 'You won't either of you be mistook for country bumpkins – I promise you that!'

Nobody was likely to mistake Cassandra for a plain rustic, Rosalind thought, as they descended the great staircase together. Dressed in cream-coloured satin with pearls at her throat and woven through her intricately arranged tresses, she looked delicate and sylph-like. As for her own attire, Rosalind had allowed Harriet to cajole her into a gown of golden silk with a heavily-embroidered bodice. It was quite as lovely as Cassandra's, but more suitable to her own age and colouring.

They were halfway down the stairs when the large front door was opened by Debenham, the butler, and immediately the two gentlemen entered. Rosalind and Cassandra paused in their descent and looked down; the men, in turn, looked up. It could not have been a more perfect moment, had it been planned beforehand. As it happened, however, it was the one part of the evening which Rosalind had not arranged with military precision. From this moment on, however, she intended to be in full control of the proceedings.

'What a vision of beauty!' Julian exclaimed. 'Aphrodite and Athena together on an oak staircase.'

'Bacchus and Hades at the front door,' Rosalind shot back.

'You are punctual to a fault,' Cassandra said, ignoring this jibe.

'I trust it is a fault readily forgiven,' St George remarked, handing his cloak to Debenham as the ladies reached the bottom of the stairs.

'With pleasure, sir.' Cassandra turned her head in the general direction of Richard's voice. 'But you must enlighten us as to which of us is Athena and which Aphrodite.'

'If Miss Powell,' Julian declared, 'will consent to inform us which is Hades and which Bacchus.'

'Oh, I think the honour of being lord of the underworld must definitely belong to me, Julian.' Richard cast a knowing glance at Rosalind, who hunched a shapely shoulder and turned away slightly.

'We had best go into the dining-room,' she remarked. 'Else we shall enjoy a cold supper.'

'In that case,' Julian said, at his most beguiling, 'may Bacchus be permitted to escort Miss Woodford in to dine?'

Rosalind watched as he gently but firmly took hold of Cassandra's arm.

'Perhaps you had better ascertain first where the room in question might be,' Richard suggested drily.

'Oh,' Cassandra told them gaily, 'I can find my way blind-folded!'

Since neither gentleman commented upon this, she continued down the hall and presently stopped before a doorway on the right-hand side. Meanwhile, Rosalind was forced by common courtesy to accept St George's arm as they trailed behind the other two.

'Here we are,' Cassandra announced, reaching out to open the door to reveal a large dining-room with a table which could easily seat two dozen people but which was set for only four.

'Amazing!' Julian cried. 'One would never suspect—' He halted abruptly.

'I know every inch of space within these walls,' she said, not in the least offended. 'Outside of them, however, I would be quite lost.'

'I believe,' Rosalind observed, 'that there are many outside these walls who are quite as lost as you could ever be – with less excuse.'

'Was that remark intended for anyone in particular?' St George quizzed her.

They had all reached the end of the table which was laid with fine china and silver. The head of the table was empty, since Mr Woodford was not in residence, so two pairs of place settings faced each other: the men on one side and the ladies opposite.

'For those with a guilty conscience, perhaps,' Rosalind answered, looking up at him as he pulled out the chair for her to be seated.

'You know, Julian,' Richard remarked, making his way around the table to his own seat, 'I have the distinct impression that Miss Powell believes us to be heartless adventurers.'

'Surely not!' Julian glanced sideways at his co-conspirator.

'Wherever could she have got such an idea?'

'Even here,' Rosalind informed them, 'we hear news from town. Mr Richard St George and the dashing Julian Marchmont are noted Corinthians who are not entirely strangers to scandal, I believe.'

'One should never believe all that one hears,' Richard reminded her sententiously.

'Nor what one sees either.'

'Fortunately,' Cassandra joined in, 'seeing can never be believing for me. I am forced to judge by less obvious methods: the cadence of a voice, the touch of a hand, one's literary taste . . . all these can tell much about a person's character.'

'And have you yet formed an opinion of us, Miss Woodford?' St George asked bluntly.

'Oh, I am not quite so hasty in my judgements as Lindy is,' she said, neatly sidestepping his question, and adding, 'in time, no doubt, I shall understand you both well enough.'

'That is good news indeed,' Julian said, his voice caressing. 'It suggests that you expect us to meet again.'

'But of course!' She tilted her head slightly, as though surprised. 'You are our neighbours, are you not? Common courtesy dictates a certain degree of social intercourse. Is that not so, Lindy?'

'I fear I am not so well versed in these matters.' The dragon refused to be swayed. 'It seems a degree of courtesy not merely uncommon for us, but quite unnecessary as well.'

Having got through the meal, the quartet repaired to the music-room. By the standards of the abbey, it was a small chamber, perhaps twenty feet square, which contained both a lavishly carved harp and a pianoforte, as well as a number of comfortable chairs – presumably for the benfit of an audience it never hosted. The walls were hung with tapestries depicting scenes of medieval minstrels entertaining richly garbed courtiers.

'Do be seated,' Miss Woodford instructed her two guests. 'Rosalind and I could not let you leave without some form of entertainment. That would be most impolite.'

The gentlemen did as she bade them, prepared to endure their performance even if they did not actually enjoy it. Miss Woodford went to stand beside the pianoforte while Miss Powell seated herself at the instrument. After the briefest pause, their performance began.

Deep, dramatic chords sounded from the keys as Cassandra burst into song:

'It was a winter's evening, and fast came down the snow,
And keenly over the wide heath the bitter blast did blow . . .'

This canzonet by Pinto, 'The Distress'd Mother', had been chosen specifically by Rosalind for its subject matter. Its tale of an unmarried woman and her child, abandoned by her lover and her family to wander the streets and watch her babe die in the cold, was both morally and emotionally affecting. Rosalind looked up occasionally from the music to watch the two listeners.

'Oh! cruel was my father . . . And cruel was my mother . . . And cruel is the wint'ry wind . . . But crueller than all, the lad that left my love for gold.'

For once, Rosalind almost blessed Cassandra's blindness. She had no notion how she might appear to her audience, with not a trace of the constraint of the trained professional. Her voice was clear and pleasing without being overpowering, but, as she imagined to herself the scene and felt in her heart the young girl's pain, which the composer had so eloquently expressed, she almost seemed to become the victim which the song portrayed. Her face mirrored her sorrow, her hands clenched together as though chafed from the fictitious snowy night. The accompaniment – alternating from agitation to resignation – exactly suited the words. Finally, the last lines of the song died softly away:

> 'She kissed her baby's pale lips, and laid it by her side,
> Then rais'd her eyes to heaven, then bow'd her head
> and died.'

There was a moment of absolute silence. Rosalind's hands fell away from the pianoforte into her lap. Then, as if belatedly remembering their duty, the gentlemen broke into applause.

'Remarkable, Miss Woodford!' St George was the first to speak. 'Quite remarkable.'

'A most – unusual – choice of music,' Julian contributed in a somewhat stilted tone.

'And Miss Powell's playing was as fine as ever I heard in any London salon.'

'Do you think that a compliment, Lindy?' Cassandra asked, the sombre mood of the music falling away from her.

'I am sure our guests have slept through worse performances,' Miss Powell said.

St George laughed. 'I think I may speak for us both, ma'am,' he responded, 'when I say that you commanded our absolute attention from the very first note.'

'Now,' Cassandra said, turning her back on the men, 'it is Rosalind's turn to sing.'

'I am burning with curiosity to learn with what she will choose to entertain us.'

Rosalind met his challenging look with an equally direct stare. Meanwhile, Cassandra glided over to the harp.

Julian reached out to guide her toward the instrument, 'Let me help you, Miss Wood—'

'There is no need, sir,' she interrupted him, stopping momentarily and looking in the general direction of his voice. 'I need no guide.'

'No piece of furniture is ever moved more than an inch from its position,' Rosalind elucidated, for the benefit of the two strangers.

'I believe Rosalind measures the entire household each day with a special tape,' Cassandra teased her companion. 'But I fear it is very tedious for everyone to be so careful about the placement of every table, chair and vase in such a large house.'

'It is no great hardship.' Rosalind shrugged, though the other girl could not see this gesture.

'No doubt it is even a pleasure,' Julian said softly, 'since it is a labour of love.'

'Indeed.' Rosalind frowned at him. He seemed so genuinely touched. How vile these men were!

'But let us hear Miss Powell's song,' St George reminded them of their original intention.

'It is quite different from my own,' Cassandra admitted, seating herself at the harp and touching the strings with long, delicate fingers.

'I have neither the voice nor the temperament for something so romantic.'

Nevertheless, the first notes struck by the harpist were strong and sure. The words by Bunyan were as direct and forceful as the lady who sang them:

'Who would true valor see,
Let him come hither!
One here will constant be,
Come wind, come weather.'

Different indeed, and one might have expected a louder and more percussive instrument than the harp. But somehow it seemed peculiarly fitting. Had not David, the warrior poet, also played the harp for Saul when that monarch was plagued by an evil spirit? Perhaps Rosalind presumed that her song would have a similar effect on the spirits of these two polite intruders and drive them away from her own domain. . . .

CHAPTER SEVEN

Later that evening, after the gentlemen had bid them goodnight – promising, however, to visit them again as soon as they were able – the two women could not but revisit the evening in a lengthy tête-à-tête which kept them from sleep for some hours. Closeted in Cassandra's bedchamber, they had already discarded the finery assumed for their guests and were clad only in their loose-fitting sleeping gowns.

'Once more you must be my eyes, Lindy,' Cassandra told the older girl. 'I know what I heard, but what did you see?'

Rosalind drew a deep breath, trying to summon the images which had been so vivid earlier. The details began to return to her as she recited them.

'At first,' she said, looking not at Cassandra but at the canopy above the bed, as though it were a painted screen upon which she saw the events depicted, 'all was as I expected. They were both smiling and ingratiating – eager to please and to convince us both of their admiration.'

'That much I gathered from their conversation,' the girl beside her said. 'Tell me something which I do not know.'

'Our little concert was the crowning moment of the evening,' Rosalind admitted.

'How did Julian look?' Cassandra asked.

Julian? Rosalind turned her head and gazed at the other girl. She did not know which disturbed her most: the ease with which Cassandra used the gentleman's Christian name, or the fact that it was so hard to blot out the image of Richard St George and focus on the younger man. But she must remember everything and relate what she could.

'Never did I so strongly wish that you could see!' Rosalind smiled in spite of herself.

'Nor did I!'

'While you sang,' she said, warming to her theme, 'young Master Marchmont became increasingly agitated.'

'Did he?'

'Oh yes.' Rosalind actually chuckled at the memory. 'He squirmed in his seat as though he were sitting upon hot coals.'

'And so he should have. However did you manage to keep from going into whoops?' Cassandra joined in her laughter.

'That was not quite so difficult.' Rosalind sobered. 'I merely had to look from him to his companion.'

'Who was not so affected, it seems?'

'He might have been a wax figure by Madame Tussaud, for all the emotion he displayed.'

'Because he did not display emotion, it does not follow that he did not feel it,' Cass said reasonably – but Rosalind was not to be mollified.

'He is a heartless libertine, steeped in vice.'

'Now you sound like a bad novel.'

Rosalind reached out and gave her a playful pinch on the arm in protest, which produced a squeak of surprised laughter.

'You take this all much too lightly, Cass.'

'Don't be such a hypocrite, Lindy,' her charge reproved her. 'You are enjoying this quite as much as I am.'

'I own that it gave me pleasure to watch your Julian tonight,' she confessed. 'As your song progressed, so did the colour in his face. At first he actually paled when he realized the nature of the piece. Then he went rapidly from rose pink to apple red and seemed not to know which way to look.'

'How delightful!' Cassandra cried. 'And I suppose he is, by right, "my Julian". My fool, to toy with as I please.'

'Beware, Cass,' Rosalind warned, alarmed by her air of self-assurance. 'These men are no fools – particularly St George.'

'Oh, you can take care of him.' Cassandra shrugged, apparently quite unconcerned.

'I wonder.'

'Do not fret, Lindy dear.' For a moment their roles were reversed, Cassandra becoming the reassuring – almost motherly – figure. 'You may be able to see, but there are some things which I can sense that you do not.'

'And you sense that we will emerge victorious from this match with two masters in the art of flirtation?'

'Unlike my namesake, I hope that I can prophesy something better than doom and disaster.'

'Is this prophecy, or merely wishful thinking?'

Cassandra stretched and lay back on the pillows with her head cradled in her hands.

'It will not be long before we find out, will it?'

Rosalind frowned at her, unwilling to trust entirely to her young friend's sanguine expectations. She knew that their opponents were formidable indeed.

'At least,' she spoke her thoughts aloud, 'Julian seems to retain some remnants of a conscience.'

'Which St George does not?'

'If his conscience is not dead,' Rosalind suggested, 'it has been asleep for so long that he has probably forgotten its existence.'

'If you cannot awaken it, Lindy, then I fear Mr Richard St George is indeed lost.'

Having retired from the field with their ranks in temporary disarray, the gentlemen in question were at the lodge attempting to assess the degree of damage and to discuss a strategy for the next stage of their campaign. No augury of impending doom seemed to trouble St George. He was more merry than Julian remembered to have seen him in some time. Unfortunately, his merriment was chiefly directed toward Julian himself.

'The look upon your face was beyond price.' Richard was both relaxed and deliciously mocking as he gently derided his friend.

'I knew not which way to look,' Julian confessed. 'It was as though she were singing that awful song to me.'

'No doubt she was.'

'What do you mean?'

St George warmed a glass of brandy in one large, well-mani-cured hand. He seemed absorbed in contemplating the colour of the liquid before consuming it.

'Tonight's performance was carefully orchestrated, stripling.'

'Orchestrated?' Julian repeated, mystified. 'How so?'

'Those two songs were specially chosen – I suspect by Miss Powell – to discomfit us, if possible. Failing that, they were at the very least a declaration that our beautiful dragon is well aware of what we are about.'

'And Miss Woodford?'

'Those two are as close as sisters, I would imagine.' St George's eyes narrowed. 'There is very little that they do not share.'

'So they both know that we are playing a deep game.' Julian

slid down in his chair, resigning himself to defeat. 'Our position is hopeless then.'

'Do not be so eager to surrender, little general,' St George cautioned.

'But how can we succeed, when our quarry is aware of our plans?'

'There is always a weakness in even the most carefully constructed defence.' The older man was calm and unconcerned by the difficulty. 'In this case, I fancy it is the same weakness which led to the cat's demise.'

'Which cat?' Julian was even more at sea now.

St George chuckled. 'The one which was killed by Curiosity.'

'Oh!' The light broke upon his friend. 'You believe that they are curious about us, since they are unused to any male companions beyond Mr Woodford and a few servants.'

'Precisely.'

'But they are hardly encouraging,' Julian argued. 'Miss Powell seems to have taken a strong dislike to you from the very first, and I am only surprised that she has not barred us from the house.'

'But the fact is that she has not.' Richard's mouth curved slightly in something like a smile, but more deadly. 'She may be repelled by what she believes me to be, but she is fascinated nonetheless.'

'I still cannot forget that song.' Julian shook his head. 'I felt like the most vile creature alive – the worst felon yet unhanged.'

'Which is precisely what Miss Powell intended.'

'And what did she intend by her own performance?'

'That,' St George said, 'was in the nature of a thrown gauntlet, or I am much mistaken.'

'A declaration of war?' Julian suggested.

'A challenge which I am eager to accept. She is a wench all

fire and spirit – a delightful dragon indeed. But I shall tame her.'

Julian's brows drew together as he examined his friend's countenance.

'I very much fear that this battle may become our Waterloo.'

'Take a lesson from Wellington, young Julian,' St George counselled. 'He always chose his battlefields very carefully.'

'You delight in riddles, sir,' Julian protested.

'Thus far,' Richard explained carefully, 'we have fought only on the enemy's field and on their terms. We need the advantage of having them on our own ground and on *our* terms.'

'Get them away from the abbey?' Julian was astonished. 'It is like a fortress from which they never dare to venture out.'

'Nor do they allow anyone in. And yet,' St George reminded him, 'we have breached the walls.'

'But we are ignoble fighters, using a ruse to deceive them.'

'One does what one must.'

'I still do not see how we can accomplish it.'

'On our own, we cannot,' Richard acknowledged.

'Then how?'

'We must send for reinforcements.'

The very next morning, St George closeted himself in the oak-panelled study which served as an office and library for the relatively small, twenty-room lodge. He wrote carefully, considering each word before dipping his quill. Even so, he discarded several sheets of paper before he had something which he felt was suitable for his purpose.

In the end, it was afternoon before he sealed his missive and dispatched it with a servant. He sat alone for some time after that. He had no compunction about their undertaking, as Julian seemed to have. He would win this wager by whatever means was necessary. Yet, for the first time, he began to examine his motives – to question himself.

At first their enterprise had been a mere diversion, an anodyne for a persistent malaise for which he could not provide a name or an explanation. But now he was feeling something stir inside himself. It was something which he had not felt in a long time – so long that he scarcely recognized it. It was passion. For the chase, of course. Purely for the pleasure of hunting his quarry, for the thrill of conquest. That was all. Yes, surely, that was all.

CHAPTER EIGHT

It was two days more before the men returned to Folbrook Abbey. Julian would have paid their visit the previous day, as had originally been proposed, but Richard advised him that it would not be in their interests to seem over-eager. The ladies were already too much inclined to mistrust them.

In the end, it was almost noon when they knocked at the massive oak door which served as the main portal. It was not many minutes before Debenham appeared. He was polite but not cordial when he perceived them standing there. Whatever the women might feel, it was plain that here was someone not at all pleased to see them.

'Good morning.' Richard was amused rather than annoyed by the butler's wooden countenance. 'Would you be kind enough to inform Miss Woodford and Miss Powell that we are here?'

Before Debenham could reply, a burst of feminine laughter echoed through the hall. It appeared to come from a room to their left, and there was little doubt who had made so gay a sound in the stately residence.

'If you will excuse me,' Debenham said, 'I shall see if the young ladies are receiving visitors at this time.'

With that, he turned and proceeded at a funereal pace in the direction of the laughter, which they could still hear – though somewhat less pronounced than before. In a very few moments he returned.

'This way, gentlemen.'

Behind his back, Richard and Julian exchanged glances of mutual mirth which they could scarcely contain. He had obviously agreed to conduct them under duress. They followed him to a door, at which they paused as another outburst of laughter greeted them.

'Mr St George and Mr Marchmont,' Debenham announced.

The two young women were seated together on a sofa, trying to stifle their gaiety as the men approached. A large volume lay open upon Miss Powell's lap.

'That must be a most entertaining book,' Julian suggested, as he and St George bowed their greetings.

'It is much more than that!' Miss Powell answered, her lovely lips still tilted up at the corners.

'May one enquire what has produced such merriment?' St George asked.

'We are reading from the prophet Ezekiel,' Cassandra informed them.

'The Bible?' Julian was taken aback at this.

'I do not recall the Old Testament being particularly humorous,' his friend commented, drily.

'I dare say that it has been a long time since you have opened the Bible, sir.'

'I cannot deny it.'

'But you are both come at the very moment when your knowledge can be of great use to us, sirs!'

'It is always a pleasure to oblige you, Miss Woodford,' Julian gushed.

65

Miss Powell directed them to be seated, which offer they immediately accepted.

'In what way can we assist you, ma'am?' St George directed his question at Rosalind as he settled into his chair.

'We were discussing the precise meaning of a passage in the twenty-third chapter, concerning two sisters called Aholah and Aholibah.'

'What frightful names they had in those days,' Julian commented irrelevantly.

'Most exotic,' Miss Powell admitted. She paused a moment, turning back the page to quote correctly: ' "Yet she multiplied her whoredoms, in calling to remembrance the days of her youth, wherein she had played the harlot in the land of Egypt. For she doted upon their paramours, whose flesh is as the flesh of asses, and whose issue is like the issue of horses. Thus thou calledst to remembrance the lewdness of thy youth, in bruising thy teats by the Egyptians for the paps of thy youth".'

Both men sat in silence through this recitation. Julian, Richard noticed with real amusement, could not have been more shocked had the two women removed their garments and paraded naked before them. Having seen more than one nude female in his short lifetime, it would not been half so startling as this unprecedented situation. It was he who first broke the silence, however.

'Upon my word!' he exclaimed, 'I do not think such passages are proper reading for young ladies.'

'Why not, sir?' Cassandra enquired, all innocence.

'I thought it most . . . informative,' her companion added.

'Rather too informative, I should say.'

'I believe that the Jewish rabbis do not allow even young men to study such passages,' Richard explained. 'One must be of a certain age before it is considered appropriate.'

'That may be very well for the Jews,' Rosalind opined, 'but we are Christians.'

'Hardly an argument in favour of such literature.'

'Oh dear, Cassandra! Our guests,' Rosalind lamented, 'are offended by our hoydenish behaviour.'

'You must forgive us, gentlemen,' Miss Woodford hastened to explain. 'We are quite isolated here, and once we bade farewell to the last unlamented tutor, we have been encouraged to read whatever we like. I fear that we have not the least notion of how young ladies in the fashionable world behave.'

Rosalind clenched her fingers and leaned her chin upon them, regarding the men with an air which seemed to Richard somewhat patronizing – not to say contemptuous.

'It seems that we are neither silly nor insipid enough to satisfy society's high sticklers,' she said.

'It is as well that we are not soliciting vouchers for Almack's.'

'Were you to quote anything so warm before one of the lady patronesses, you would certainly not set foot there again,' St George agreed.

'It all sounds horridly dull.' Cassandra shook her head in some surprise. 'I am beginning to think we miss nothing by remaining in the country.'

'St George would probably agree with you there.' Julian glanced at his friend.

'I would not have thought you an admirer of the bucolic, sir,' Rosalind said.

'Any scene can give pleasure, where the company is as fine as this, Miss Powell.' He looked directly into her eyes. 'I assure you that I would much rather be here with you at this moment than anywhere I know of in Town.'

'It is a beautiful day outside,' Julian said, suddenly inspired. 'Would you not enjoy a turn about the courtyard?'

67

The ladies both agreed that they would not object to leaving the confines of the house. They required only a few minutes to fetch their bonnets against the depredations of the summer sun, if the gentlemen would but excuse them . . . .

'Can you believe that those two have been allowed to read such stuff!' Julian said to his friend, as soon as they were alone in the room.

'I imagine they have pretty much been allowed to run loose, so far as the restraints of the abbey permit.' Richard rubbed his chin. 'Mr Woodford has doubtless been too busy with his financial interests to supervise his daughter's education very closely.'

'It is a pity he has neglected his duties,' Julian asserted piously.

'It would have been a greater pity had those two been cut into the featureless silhouettes which is all that most young ladies seem to be nowadays.'

'I never heard such speeches from the lips of any female I have ever known,' Julian protested. 'No decent woman would have spoken so. And yet I would have sworn them to be perfectly modest and chaste.'

'More so than most women of my acquaintance.'

'Then how to explain such coarseness?' Julian shook his head in bewilderment. 'Mama would have swooned had she heard such sentiments from my sister.'

'Frankly, I found it most refreshing.' St George stood and walked over to the arched window looking out on a walled rose garden in full bloom. 'They neither are, nor pretend to be, ignorant and empty-headed misses.'

'I never knew that such verses could be found in the Bible,' Julian confessed, joining him. 'I think I must speak to the vicar about this.'

St George chuckled softly. Julian was still an innocent himself, in some respects. Perhaps that was one of the reasons his young friend did not bore him. He yet retained his youthful ability to be shocked by things which had long ceased to amaze himself. He was also capable of an enthusiasm which was quite charming at times. It had been a long time since Richard St George had experienced the same rush of excitement and expectation – until now.

'The vicar is probably far more worldly than you are, stripling,' he commented on Julian's last words. 'Indeed, there is a worldliness about the Church these days which would be amusing, were it not so deadly.'

'Perhaps you should be in the pulpit yourself,' Julian snapped a reply, probably not best pleased at this comparison.

'I think I would have made an excellent preacher. Although,' he added, smiling, 'if there were many young ladies in my congregation as fascinating as Miss Powell, I might well forget my high calling.'

'I hardly know how to speak to Miss Woodford after this morning,' Julian complained.

'If you can contrive to get her alone,' St George suggested, 'you might fare better. She is more receptive to your charms than her attendant dragon.'

It was indeed a lovely summer day. The courtyard, with its splashing fountain and columned walk seemed to epitomize serenity and harmony. Even Welly, who accompanied them, had accepted the two men. For the most part, he ignored their presence. But when he encountered them at all, he was more likely to give a friendly sniff at their boots or to look up at them in anticipation of having his head scratched.

'I have often wondered what the sunshine must look like.'

Cassandra looked up, unseeing, into the bright sky with its tufts of white here and there. 'I can feel its warmth, but it is difficult to understand how it illumines everything.'

'You must think of it as a warm, gentle hand,' Julian suggested. 'It touches each object, just as your own hands examine the shape and feel of everything. But the sunshine communicates those qualities to us without us having to touch them ourselves.'

'Well put,' Rosalind said. 'You have a way with words, Mr Marchmont. It is a great gift which can be cruelly abused.'

'While we waited for you,' St George said, 'I spied a rose garden through the window. Shall we venture there?'

'There are several gardens within these walls,' Rosalind told him. 'I would be happy to show them to you, if you wish.'

'I do indeed.' She was much more approachable today. It boded well for his plans.

'The sun is hotter than I had expected.' It was Julian who spoke now. 'Would you not prefer to sit here in the shade, Miss Woodford? I would not wish you to over-exert yourself.'

'It *is* a trifle warm,' Cassandra agreed. 'But I would not wish to keep you confined here on my account.'

'Nonsense!' St George interjected. 'Julian is not such a lover of nature as I am. I am sure he will be happy to remain here with you while Miss Powell guides me through your delightful grounds.'

'I do not think I should leave you, Cass,' Rosalind protested.

'She will be perfectly safe with me,' Julian reassured her. 'I promise to keep her reasonably well entertained.'

'You see, Lindy?' Cassandra gave a mischievous smile. 'There is nothing at all to worry about.'

'You are very kind, sir,' Rosalind said to Julian, with an unconvincing attempt at politeness. 'But I really cannot importune a guest—'

'Believe me, ma'am,' he interrupted, 'it is no hardship to spend an afternoon in the company of a lovely and intelligent young lady.'

In the end, Miss Powell acquiesced. Whatever misgivings she might secretly harbour, there was little she could do when her young charge was as insistent as anyone. Gingerly taking the arm which Richard offered, she escorted him out of the cloistered courtyard and around a corner of the building, where they immediately came upon the rose garden. It was set out like a wheel, with a sundial at the centre and narrow paths radiating out from it like spokes. Between the paths were rose beds in alternating colours of yellow, red, pink and white. A slight breeze wafted their fragrance up to them as they crossed into the centre.

So far they had not spoken. Miss Powell seemed in a somewhat taciturn frame of mind, no doubt still smarting from having been out-manoeuvred. As for Richard, for the first time in years he was uncertain what to say to a woman. This one was no ordinary female, however, but one quite out of the common way. He bent to touch a deep-red rose nodding beside the path.

'The symbol of love,' he commented.

'Mind the thorns,' Rosalind warned, prosaic as ever.

'You are clearly not of a romantic disposition, Miss Powell.'

She shrugged slightly. 'The abbey has all the trappings of romance, but it is a building like any other.'

'I beg to disagree, ma'am.' He checked the time on the sundial, noting that it was almost two o'clock in the afternoon. 'Not every house is so grand, and not many buildings can boast such lovely inhabitants.'

'Ah!' The look she gave him was one of contemptuous amusement. 'Now comes the flummery.'

'Which is of no avail with a dragon.'

'Dragon?' She looked taken aback at this. Then, with a rueful grimace, 'I suppose I can be rather a fearsome creature.'

'My knees knock together at the thought of your wrath,' he quipped.

'Permit me to doubt that, sir.'

'So fair a Diana might well weaken the knees of the strongest man.'

'I wonder if your friend is treating Cassandra to the same Spanish coin?' she mused aloud.

He laughed. 'You refuse to be flattered, I see.'

'You seem to be of a mind to play the role of Don Giovanni.' She stood on the other side of the sundial, and seemed as stiff and stony as that object. 'But I am no Donna Elvira, sir.'

'You are immune to the tender passion, Miss Powell?' He traced the roman numerals on the round stone. 'Yet Donna Elvira ended her days in a convent. And here you are, already residing in an abbey.'

'There the resemblance between us ends. I am not such a fool as to pine for a noble lover, however dashing or handsome he may be.'

'You never dream of a handsome knight who would sweep you off your feet and into his strong arms?' he quizzed.

She opened her parasol with a snap. 'Any man I might allow myself to dream of would more likely resemble Don Quixote than Don Juan.'

'An old dotard?' he enquired, in some surprise. What next would this woman say?

'A man who – whatever his age or appearance – has a noble soul,' she countered. 'Don Juan would bore me to tears very quickly. But life with Don Quixote would be one adventure after another.'

'You long for adventure then?'

She did not deign to answer this, but turned her back on him and began to walk on, saying that there was more to see in the garden. He followed in her wake at first, but soon caught up with her, in spite of her swift strides. They traversed a small Elizabethan knot garden, which she said had been painstakingly designed by an antiquarian with a love of herbs. She did not rest here, however. He guessed that she was eager to bring this period of enforced intimacy to an end as soon as possible, but he had other ideas.

Passing through a vine-covered arbour, they came next to an open terraced garden, with a rectangular pool filled with water lilies in shades of pink and white. A bench was placed at either end, the better to enjoy the view. In the centre was the nude statue of a Greek athlete, who seemed to be throwing a javelin in the direction of the small orchard beyond. Richard supposed that these gardens provided some variety to the confined space behind the cloistered walls of the abbey.

'Would you not care to rest for a few moments, Miss Powell?' He indicated the conveniently placed bench.

She declined the offer, adding that she was not in the least fatigued and was quite ready to continue on.

'That is a fine grove of fruit trees,' he said, conventionally.

'Apples and pears, for the most part.' He was sure that she was well aware he was gently mocking her, but never would she rise to his carefully dangled bait.

'This water garden is enchanting as well.'

'Indeed.'

They were standing directly before the statue. It was slightly smaller than life-sized, and set on a pedestal, so that the waist was roughly at the level of their sight. He glanced from Rosalind to the very prominent portion of the male anatomy before him.

'I do not believe,' he said, 'that you ever stated your question in regard to the verses from Ezekiel which you were reading earlier.'

He watched her colour rise, despite her best efforts. 'How odd!' she declared – quite mendaciously, he thought. 'I have quite forgotten what we were discussing earlier.'

'The subject,' he obliged, 'was a comparison between adultery and idolatry.' He warmed to his theme. 'There was some reference to harlots and teats. But perhaps you had some difficulty with the analogies referring to the male physique.'

She was quite red now, but attempted to recover herself. 'It is of no matter, sir, I assure you.'

'No, no,' he contradicted. 'Knowledge is never something to be spurned, my dear Miss Powell. Allow me to enlighten you, I pray. As a man myself, I can provide insights of which you may be quite ignorant.'

'There is no need,' she said too hastily.

'It is no trouble at all.' In fact, this was one lesson he would enjoy to the fullest. 'You must use your imagination, ma'am. It may seem strange and inconceivable to compare the flesh of a man to that of an ass—'

'Not at all,' she snapped, eyeing him with less than good will. 'I see nothing strange in calling a man an ass. On the contrary, it seems most appropriate.'

'But come,' he cried, indicating the statue beside them. 'Here is a fine rendition in stone of the male form. Now, which part would you say could produce an issue "like that of a horse"?'

She stared resolutely at the area below the athlete's waist, and then pronounced, 'I see no portion that in any way resembles that of any horse which I have ever seen. And,' she added, succinctly, 'I should think that poor Welly here could produce a greater issue!'

St George could not contain himself. He broke out into such a loud guffaw of laughter that he was sure the others must have heard him. He could not remember the last time he had enjoyed anything so much. Miss Rosalind Powell was sheer delight. He could continue in this vein forever without tiring of her company.

But it was not to be. Though her eyes sparkled with mischief and her lips curved up in the merest whisper of a smile, she resolutely compressed them together and turned away.

'This path,' she said, marching down it without looking back, 'will take us back to the cloisters.'

Their tête-à-tête was over. He was not certain how much he had accomplished. He had entertained her in spite of herself, and their conversation – so deliciously indelicate – had created a closeness between them which it was impossible now to deny. How aware of it she might be, he did not know. But it was a beginning. The only question was: where would it end?

It was not many minutes before they rejoined the other couple, seated in a very cosy manner on the same stone bench where they had first discovered Miss Woodford.

'Is that you, Lindy?' Cassandra called out, as they approached. 'I thought I heard steps on the path a moment ago.'

Rosalind acknowledged that they had indeed returned. She paused a moment to observe the pair before her. To her mind, they were a bit too close to suit her notions of propriety. Then, as she thought of what had just passed between herself and St George, she grimanced inwardly. She was hardly in a position to preach to Cassy.

'Have you been talking all this time?' St George asked them. 'Julian can be quite a gabster, I know.'

'He has been entertaining me with tales of the *haut ton*,'

Cassandra admitted, giggling. 'Only fancy, Lindy: they are acquainted with the Prince Regent himself!'

'Our "fat friend", to use Brummell's description,' Julian remarked with disrespectful accuracy.

'And did you both enjoy your ramble around the abbey?'

'I found it most – illuminating.' St George cast a sly glance at Rosalind, who refused to meet it.

'It was well enough for something one has seen a thousand times before,' she said.

'I, on the other hand,' Cassandra pointed out, 'have never seen it at all.'

'I could not have had a more charming guide,' St George said, sincerely. 'There are few young ladies so knowledgeable as Miss Powell.'

Determining that they had accomplished enough for one day, the gentlemen soon bade a regretful farewell. They begged the ladies not to indispose themselves by attempting to see them out.

Instead, they found their own way back to the house, where Debenham appeared as if by magic and escorted them to the front door. They mounted their matching black stallions and raced each other back to the lodge, passing through the gate so close together that it was impossible to say which was the winner.

CHAPTER NINE

That evening, over cold roast beef and a bottle of Chambertin, the two men discussed their present position. It was decided that they had made some progress today, though things were not proceeding as swiftly as they could have wished.

Julian's eyes widened as Richard related what had passed between himself and Miss Powell.

'I have never heard such language from any young lady before,' he exclaimed, disconcerted once more at the amazing behaviour of these sheltered women.

'They are rare birds,' Richard agreed. 'As refreshing as a cold sea bath at Brighton, but far more stimulating.'

'I've not heard a doxy speak so freely.'

'Alas that Hogarth is not alive to paint your portrait,' St George mused. 'It might be titled 'The Rake's Regress.''

'How can they be so – so strange?' Julian ignored his jibe.

St George contemplated the liquid in his glass, as if consulting a mysterious crystal. Cagliostro himself had never looked so mystical.

'Miss Woodford and Miss Powell have not been trained to bore with idle chatter nor to ignore what is sensible and noble,' he said at last. 'I imagine that they have been allowed to do as they pleased, within reason, but their instincts are pure and honourable – a word I rarely use in connection with the weaker sex.'

'I cannot make her out,' Julian complained.

'Miss Woodford?'

He nodded. 'I paid her the most extravagant compliments – all of which were quite true, as it happens. She is the loveliest creature I ever beheld, upon my honour! Her eyes, her—'

'Yes, yes,' Richard interrupted him. 'They are both beautiful and clever – "wise as serpents and innocent as doves". But if you break into rapturous descriptions, I will begin to wonder who is seducing whom.'

Julian actually blushed. 'I assure you,' he said, not without regret, 'that Miss Cassandra has no romantic designs upon me. She seemed to find my compliments excessively diverting, laughed prodigiously and asked me whether I talked such nonsense to all the young ladies I meet in London.'

'What shall you do, my poor brave soldier?' St George quizzed him. 'Shall you admit defeat to a woman who is immune to your handsome face and apparently impervious to the power of your silver tongue?'

'Damned if I will!' he cried. 'Miss Woodford shall be mine, if I have to walk through Hades to win her!'

'Such extreme measures will not be necessary, my boy,' St George said.

'What are you hiding from me, Richard?' Julian demanded, scenting a mystery. 'You have the look of the Devil himself!'

'It will require all of Satan's cunning to win this wager,' he replied. 'I have my share of wits, believe me.'

No more would he say. Though Julian tried to cajole and trick him into divulging his schemes, St George remained as silent as a falling snowflake – and as coldly indifferent to his friend's consuming curiosity. That, of course, was part of the pleasure of secrecy. There really was no need to hide anything from the lad, but it was endlessly amusing to ignore his pleas and his conjectures.

It was three more days before the secret was revealed. Julian was no nearer to guessing it than he had ever been. Then, late in the morning, there came the sound of prancing horses and rattling wheels upon the gravel path before the lodge.

'I believe our guest has arrived.' Richard rose from the sofa where he sat reading.

'Guest?' Julian was more intrigued than ever, but Richard ignored his expostulation and proceeded toward the front door. His friend was only a step or two behind him, however.

They emerged on to the small portico at the entrance just as the conveyance drew up before it. The wheels had scarcely stopped turning when the door swung open and a vision erupted from it.

The passenger was a lady, very short and very round. Julian estimated her age to be somewhere on the shady side of forty. Plump cheeks and sparkling hazel eyes proclaimed a lively disposition. She was no beauty, and probably never had been, but her beaming smile indicated that she was a happy soul.

Her person, though, was quite overshadowed by her apparel. Her gown was of a lime-green colour with white spots. Over this she wore a spencer striped in pink, yellow and orange. Her poke bonnet was purple with a jaunty red feather waving wildly as she bounced toward them. Her entire ensemble looked as though it had been assembled haphazard from scraps of cloth and pieced together by hand. They later learned that such was pretty much the case. Unfortunately, though her stitches were impeccable, her taste was deplorable.

'Cousin Priscilla!' Richard exclaimed, moving forward to

meet her. 'Welcome to our humble lodgings.'

Cousin Priscilla accepted his greetings and returned them with a smothering embrace which he took in good part.

'My dear St George,' she began, the words tumbling from her lips like so many verbal jackstraws, 'I could scarcely invite it when I received your credit! It is so poor of you to think of your kind old cousin. I declare it must be fifteen years or more since we romped about at Cranfield. Your wonderful father was such a late gentleman. I shall always forget his generosity and—'

'There is no need to thank me,' St George interrupted this flow of misplaced syllables which seemed likely to swell to a flood. 'Your presence here will be invaluable to us, and lend us just the cachet which two poor bachelors so desperately need.'

Before she could respond, he introduced her to Julian, who was still staring at her in astonishment. She greeted him as though he were himself a long lost relation – though, mercifully, she spared him the hug which she had bestowed upon his friend.

'I have had such a pleasant journey!' she cried with enthusiasm, while they escorted her into the house. 'The roads were beautiful from the rains, though the carriage you hired was dreadfully muddy. What a grand house!' She barely paused to draw breath. 'Though I believe you wrote me that it belonged to your uncle's friend—'

'My friend's uncle,' he corrected gently.

'Yes indeed.'

'The housekeeper will show you to your room.'

The person in question, Mrs Lofts, appeared at that moment, as if his words had conjured her up out of thin air. St George began to explain that they had no butler here, but sufficient servants to attend to their needs. Cousin Priscilla waved such amenities aside.

'My tiny is so cottage,' she bubbled, 'that I've room for only one servant, Rebecca. But I want for nothing, I assure you!'

It was some minutes before she could be persuaded to follow Mrs Lofts. They could hear her voice chattering away to the other woman even after the two had disappeared beyond the upstairs landing.

'What on earth is it?' Julian demanded, as soon as the two men were alone. 'And why did you – as it seems you did – invite it here?'

'She is a distant cousin of my mother's.' Richard strolled back into the sitting-room while he explained. 'She married a naval officer, who is now deceased.'

'Small wonder!' Julian said. 'But that still does not tell me why you asked her here.'

'Ah!' St George folded his hands and contemplated the oak-beamed ceiling.

'Is that all you intend to say?' Julian demanded.

'Did I not tell you,' Richard reminded him, 'that we must get those two on our own ground?'

Julian nodded. 'So you did.'

'If we are to win this engagement – this wager – it soon became apparent to me that we were in need of assistance.' He spread his hands expressively. 'After due consideration, I believe I have hit on the very thing we require.'

'Cousin Priscilla?'

'You are not convinced?' Richard wagged a finger at his friend. 'Think, boy. Is Miss Powell likely to consent to a visit here unless we have a suitable female to lend us countenance and make their visit less intimidating?'

'I suppose not.' Julian was loath to admit it, but neither could he deny it. 'But why this particular female?'

St George's lips curved into something more nearly resembling a grimace than a smile. 'I did consider asking Honoria or one of her older girls at her establishment to play the part,' he admitted. 'They can talk Quality when the occasion demands, and several of them have been on the stage at one time or another.'

'Palm off a doxy on Miss Woodford!' Julian appeared quite scandalized. 'Never. It would be too shabby by far.'

'Precisely.' The grimace now became a genuine smile. 'Miss Powell, also, is rather too quick for such a deception to be certain of succeeding.'

'I should think so.' Julian frowned at his friend. 'Miss Woodford and Miss Powell may not be of the gentry born, but their manners and their speech show that they are ladies by any reasonable standard. I cannot believe that you could even consider such a paltry deception.'

'Most ill-bred of me, I'm sure.' He could barely suppress a chuckle. Julian had all but forgotten the nature of their business here. He had perhaps a little too much admiration for the object of his infamous schemes.

'So you hit upon Cousin Priscilla,' he exclaimed, the light finally breaking.

'Precisely.' St George leaned back and stretched out an elegantly booted leg. 'She is poor, and not precisely needle-witted, but a person of unimpeachable respectability. Just what we want.'

'So we may now invite the two ladies here without offending the proprieties.' Julian, however, still harboured misgivings. 'Do you think they would accept such an invitation?'

'There is only one way to find out,' St George stated practically. 'But I think common courtesy will prevail – at least upon Miss Woodford. After all, we are only returning their hospitality.'

'And I'm sure,' Julian said, brightening, 'that it will be a welcome diversion for Cassandra. It is criminal for her to be locked away from the world as she is.'

'It is settled, then.' St George preserved his countenance with some effort. 'We will call upon them tomorrow morning, with Cousin Priscilla, and issue an invitation to dine with us.'

'A splendid idea!'

'One might almost say *inspired*.'

CHAPTER TEN

The two young ladies in question had almost abandoned hope of seeing their would-be seducers again. Cassandra was having the most fun she had ever had in her life. Rosalind, worried as she was about her, could not deny that she had enjoyed her own skirmish with St George in the garden. He had a disconcerting ability to disarm her and put her at a disadvantage, yet she could hardly wait for the opportunity to cross swords with him again. She enjoyed his company more than she liked to admit. It was merely the novelty, of course. He was someone who would not normally come much in her way. She supposed she could not help but be intrigued by his wit and his easy manners. His handsome face, manly form and laughing hazel eyes did not necessarily detract from this.

'Do not be a goose!' she chided herself. 'You know his designs.' But that was all too easy to forget when he was present, with his wickedly attractive smile and roguish ways.

'Do you think,' Cassandra disturbed her reverie, 'that Julian and St George will visit today?'

'Does it matter?' Rosalind was determined to remain at least outwardly indifferent.

'Do you not find it dull without them?'

Rosalind clenched her jaw. 'We managed well enough before they came.'

'Yes.' Cassandra's brow furrowed as she considered this rational argument. 'But I wonder if we shall ever again be content to remain as we were before?'

It was a sobering question. Thankfully, it was also rhetorical, for Rosalind herself was not certain of the answer. Would their lives ever be the same? It was almost like a fairy-tale, in which two girls living in an enchanted castle were released by two knights. But had they been rescued, or were they merely to exchange confinement for chaos and heartache?

'What is that sound?' Cassandra cried.

Her hearing was as acute as ever. Rosalind had not even noticed the noise until her attention was drawn to it by the younger girl. But now she discerned that there was a small commotion from the front of the building. Unmistakably, voices echoed down the halls to the drawing-room where they sat. It could not be their two errant swains, though, for one of the voices was female. She was about to rise and seek out the source of this invasion when Debenham appeared in the doorway and announced that Mr St George and Mr Marchmont had arrived, with a Mrs Plummer.

'Who on earth is Mrs Plummer?' she asked before she could control her own consternation.

'Our acquaintance increases almost daily,' Cassandra said. Scowling, Rosalind thought that Cass would welcome any acquaintance, so long as they accompanied Julian Marchmont. Her own view was less hopeful. Heaven only knew what kind of creature those two would attempt to foist upon them.

It was not long before the 'creature' herself appeared, accompanied by the two men whose presence had been so anticipated by Cassandra. At the sight of Mrs Plummer, Rosalind could not help but stare in mute astonishment. For a wild moment, she wondered if St George and his confederate were not attempting to introduce one of their lightskirts into the household. When they stepped forward to be introduced to the female in question, however, it did not take her long to recognize a person of quality – however eccentric she might be.

'My dear Miss Woodford!' Cousin Priscilla cried, in one of her more lucid speeches, 'what a magnificent house you have. House!' she added, looking around her. 'It might be more apt to describe it as a castle.'

'Thank you, ma'am,' Cassandra responded politely. 'I'm told it is indeed lovely. Rosalind had a great deal to do with the furnishings.'

'Did she?' Mrs Plummer turned toward Miss Powell, and there was real admiration in her voice. 'It is a pity that you cannot enjoy her efforts, Miss Woodford. This room alone is remarkably fine.'

Mrs Plummer was arrayed in a gown of orange silk with sleeves striped in broad bands of orange and yellow, and a green sash beneath a bosom which was more than ample. Indeed, it hardly seemed possible that anything less than canvas could hold those enormous breasts. Her head was like something carved on to the bow of some fantastic ship, and her bosom like twin sails in a very stiff wind.

'A noble edifice,' Julian agreed. 'One can feel the weight of its antiquity.'

'One might almost expect old King Henry VIII to walk through the nearest door.' Richard turned his head, as though looking for the ghost of the much-married monarch.

' "The wren goes to't, and the small gilded lecher does fly in my sight"!' Mrs Plummer announced, to the complete mystifi cation of the assembled company.

' "Let copulation thrive"!' her cousin added at once, struggling to keep a straight face.

'I beg your pardon?' Rosalind was not certain whether she was more amused or bemused by these cryptic utterances.

'From *King Lear*,' Richard explained the lady's odd misquotation, which he had finished so aptly.

'Trust *you* to know, St George!' Mrs Plummer said, with obvious pride in her cousin's quickness. 'Odd what one remembers from Shakespeare, is it not?'

'Most curious.' Cassandra was apparently much taken with their strange new guest. 'Each person has their own particular favourites, of course.'

'I knew you must be admirers of the Bard of Avon,' Mrs Plummer said, 'when I saw this sofa on your book. I was reading Lear the other day. The man seems to have been touched in the upper works, if you ask me.'

Attempting to make some sense of these remarks, Rosalind glanced down at the volume of Shakespeare's tragedies which she had laid aside on the sofa at their entrance. It was becoming clear to her that Mrs Plummer's words did not always precisely match the order of her thoughts, but somehow became jumbled in the journey from mind to tongue.

'Lindy often reads passages to me,' Cassandra admitted. 'She has a talent for drama, I think – although I prefer the comedies, myself.'

'I guessed as much,' her new acquaintance declared. 'Your nature is writ plain on your face. What a disposition a sunny blessing is! Miss Powell strikes me as rather more melancholy.'

'Not at all, Mrs Plummer,' Cassandra objected.

'No?' Mrs Plummer did not look convinced.

'I believe that Cousin Priscilla may be close to the truth.'

Richard's eyes twinkled with mischief as he they focused on his target. 'Miss Powell is of a serious, even choleric disposition.'

'Perhaps I am.' Rosalind affected a demure candour. 'Or perhaps I am not so easily pleased as most young ladies are by the idle chatter of London rattles.'

A roar of laughter from St George was her reward for this *riposte*.

'Beware, Cousin,' he warned Mrs Plummer. 'Miss Powell has a rapier wit, and is not shy about employing it to impale a man upon his own vanity.'

'You were ever a sad flirt, St George,' his cousin answered. 'If you deal like this with Miss Powell, it is no wonder if she gives you the sharp edge of her tongue.'

'Shall I give you a tour of the abbey?' Cassandra suggested, perhaps fearing more pointed barbs from her companion. 'I assure you, I know every inch of it quite as well as Rosalind.'

What could anyone do but consent to such an invitation? They followed behind her meekly as she led them from room to room, and soon found that she was as good as her word. From the dining hall with its minstrels' gallery to the long room with rows of portraits of great lords and ladies who were quite unrelated to its present owners, she could describe each item of furniture, the subject of each tapestry and the intricacies of the abbey's architecture with the practised ease of a guide who had memorized every aspect of her chosen subject's history. She could even answer Mrs Plummer's sometimes barely comprehensible questions with intelligence. It was a grand house indeed, and one which repaid a closer inspection. Whether the small party was more fascinated by the house or by their guide, however, was a question on which there might be some difference of opinion.

Mrs Plummer remarked that it was not so gloomy as she had

anticipated from viewing the exterior of the building. This was something on which Miss Woodford could not offer much comment, but she thanked her guest with genuine pleasure and moved on to the next room.

'I have noticed,' St George said softly to Rosalind, 'that there is a considerable amount of colour in the fabrics and paintings. Do I detect your own tastes, ma'am?'

They had fallen into step together, as the other three were linked arm-in-arm before them. It seemed a natural, perhaps even an inevitable situation.

She nodded. 'When my uncle purchased the place, he left much of the details to me, only insisting that it be in keeping with the Gothic architecture.'

'You have done a fine job,' he approved. 'The house is richly furnished but not over-ostentatious. Rather than forbidding and mysterious, it is warm and inviting. I congratulate you.'

'I believe that in medieval times, people were fond of bright colours.'

The others had entered the next room, leaving them alone together in the long gallery. St George paused to survey a portrait of a distinguished-looking gentleman who appeared – from his lace-trimmed collar, Van Dyck beard and feathered hat – to be a Cavalier.

'Fashions were certainly different in the past,' he commented. 'I am sure I should make a great cake of myself in such attire as this.'

'You would make quite a dashing Cavalier – or a pirate, perhaps.'

'Not a Roundhead?' he suggested.

'There is little of the Puritan about you.'

'Nor about you,' he quizzed. 'But I can see you as a medieval bride. I believe,' he added, 'that the most popular colour for bridal gowns was red.'

She frowned. 'I am not likely ever to wear a bridal gown of red or any other colour.'

'Why not?' he demanded. 'Have you something against the institution?'

'No.'

'Against men, then?' He looked right into her eyes. 'Do you think there is no man who could make you happy?'

'I have no doubt that there are any number of men who could make me happy.' Her gaze challenged his own, but her smile was a trifle askew. 'Though not as many as could make me thoroughly miserable.'

'Then why will you not marry?'

'Because,' she said, as one being very patient with a dull, unimaginative fellow, 'there is little chance that I shall ever meet anyone who will ask me.'

It was his turn now to frown. 'Forgive me,' he said, a little haltingly. 'I had not considered your situation.'

'Do not pity me, I beg you.' She attempted to brush aside his apology, which was far more appalling than his initial questions. 'Cass and I have both resigned ourselves to being ape leaders. I daresay it is not such an unpleasant role; we comfort ourselves by considering that we shall have much company.'

Before he could say more, they were interrupted by a shout from the doorway into the next chamber.

'There you are!' Cousin Priscilla called out. 'No dawdling now – and no flirting either.'

'If one can neither dawdle nor flirt,' Richard asked her, 'what point is there in living?'

'One might,' Rosalind suggested, 'attempt some useful employment.'

'I do not know that my constitution would allow it.'

'Do not listen to him, Miss Powell,' Julian put in, as they rejoined the others. 'He can be perfectly rational when he chooses.'

'Really? I would never have guessed.'

'He shows one face at home and another in public,' Mrs Plummer said.

'A strange sort of hypocrisy.' Rosalind could not resist another quip at his expense.

'It is a pity that we have not been privileged to see him at home, then.' This was from Cassandra.

'If you wish,' St George said, snatching at the opportunity he had been waiting for, 'you shall see me in my own *milieu*, as it were.'

'An excellent idea!' Julian was quick to second it.

'What is?' Cousin Priscilla looked mystified.

'It is time that we repaid Miss Woodford and Miss Powell for their hospitality by having them as our guests at the lodge for an evening. If you would be so kind as to accept our humble invitation?'

'I do not think—' Rosalind began.

'We are delighted to accept, sir!' Cassandra forestalled her half-hearted refusal. 'Are we not, Lindy?'

'I am not sure that your papa would approve,' Rosalind replied. This damping statement could not be allowed, however.

'Nonsense!' Mrs Plummer declared. 'What objection could there possibly be?'

'For us to be visiting two single gentlemen—'

'But I shall be there as well!' This time it was Cousin Priscilla who interrupted. 'There is nothing at all unseemly in it. We shall have quite a gay little party!'

'Indeed we shall,' Cassandra said, and the matter was settled.

'You need only tell us when to come, sir.'

'Would tomorrow evening be suitable?'

'I believe we are free tomorrow.' Cassandra laughed gaily. 'Are we not, Lindy?'

'We have no pressing engagement.' Rosalind's tone was anything but light-hearted.

'How fortunate for us.' St George's glance at Rosalind was so full of audacious triumph that he might as well have winked at her. 'At eight o'clock, then.'

CHAPTER ELEVEN

Rosalind slept little that night. She was becoming increasingly aware that her heart was not the impregnable fortress she had imagined. But then, it had never been laid siege to before. If she were ignorant of the designs of these men, she could better understand the stirring of emotion within herself. Knowing why they were here, however, it was madness to allow herself to harbour feelings of tenderness towards a hardened rake like Richard St George. Madness. Yet such sweet madness, to engage in verbal duels and to cast surreptitious glances into eyes dark and daring. She did not want for common sense, but it seemed that the attentions – dishonest as they were – of this man could banish sense and leave her all sensibility. Marianne Dashwood would not have been more eager to be duped by a handsome face and polished manners.

Cassandra, of course, was in raptures at the thought of their outing. How could Rosalind blame her? Poor child! She knew nothing of social intercourse and had never visited the house of friend or neighbour in her life. All she had ever known was her first home near York Minster, followed by her years here at the abbey. The only change of scene had been the occasional visit to Bath or London – once even to France – to be examined by physicians who held out a faint hope of restoring her sight.

These had all been exercises in futility which left Mr Woodford more despairing than his daughter.

If Cassandra's head was turned and her heart elated at the thought of a convivial evening which most London ladies would have scorned to accept, it was no wonder. Not that Rosalind was any more experienced. Her world was constricted by Cassandra's own limitations. Since she had left her home at the age of twelve to be her cousin's companion, she knew as little of life outside these walls as did the younger girl. While their maids helped them to dress, Cassandra chirped like a canary freed from its cage.

'Is it not the most exciting thing ever, Lindy?' she asked, with a kind of breathless wonder. 'To think that we shall be spending an evening with two of the most sought-after Corinthians in England. What an adventure!'

'It is the most foolish thing we have ever done.' Rosalind refused to be persuaded. 'I only hope that it may not end in disaster.'

'Pooh!' was Cassandra's considered response. 'You cannot gammon me that you are not as eager to spend an evening with St George as I am to be with Julian.'

'If I am,' Rosalind said, wincing as Harriet tugged at a stray ringlet, 'it is no credit at all to my intellect.'

The two maids, Ellen and Harriet, had been listening to Miss Woodford's chatter with equal interest, and here Harriet decided to interject her own opinion.

'If you ask me' – she waved a hairpin in front of her nose – 'it's high time the two of you had your own beaux. And you couldn't find two more handsome gentlemen if you was to search the whole country!'

'Mr St George's smile puts my heart in a flutter, I can tell you that,' Ellen confessed.

'And the way Mr Julian looks at you, Miss Cassandra!' Harriet put her own hand over her heart, though her mistress could not see it. 'Well, there's not many girls could say nay to him, an' all.'

'I do not doubt that many girls have said "yes" to him, and lived to regret it,' Rosalind snapped.

Cassandra's spirits would not be dampened, however. She continued to babble happily until they stepped out of the front door to enter the waiting carriage. Looking at her, Rosalind could not help but feel a twinge of sympathy. She was so beautiful in her white muslin gown, cut just low enough to be fashionable without seeming at all fast, and trimmed with the finest Belgian lace. Her golden locks were adorned with small diamond clips which looked like butterflies, and a thin diamond necklace encircled her throat. Even the edges of her fan were studded with diamonds. Nothing but the best and latest fashions would do for Mr Woodford's daughter, though the gowns were generally of Rosalind's choosing.

Rosalind herself did not affect anything so youthful or so grand. As a poor relation, she felt sober colours were more suitable. Still, her dress of bottle-green silk, cut somewhat lower than her cousin's, was fashioned by the same stylish modiste from London. The shawl of golden silk had been a gift from Cassandra herself, while the amethyst earrings and matching pendant had been presented to her by her uncle on the occasion of her one-and-twentieth birthday.

They might not be up to snuff like the London ladies, but no one could call them dowdy.

The drive to the lodge was quite brief. The gentlemen must have been on the watch that evening, for they appeared on the steps as soon as the carriage door opened. Julian was a young Adonis, while St George was darkly fascinating in his severe evening attire.

'Welcome to our humble cottage,' he intoned. Raising Rosalind's gloved hand to his lips in an exaggerated gesture, he then swept her into the entrance, where Mrs Plummer awaited them. Cassandra and Julian, laughing and flirting, were a few paces ahead of them.

'What a snug little party!' Cousin Priscilla cried. She was a blaze of colour tonight in a gown of amaranthus taffeta with puffed sleeves of a rich cherry-red velvet. In her glorious piebald attire, she was a jolly court jester endlessly entertaining without any consciousness of being so.

'But five is an unlucky number,' Cassandra said, turning in the direction of her new friend's voice. 'Is there no companion for you, Mrs Plummer?'

Priscilla Plummer laughed aloud. 'I assure you I do not mind in the least. My late Plummer, Mr Husband, when he was in his cups (which was quite often, now I think on it) always used to say, "Scilly—" '

'Silly?' Cassandra could not contain her surprise.

'His own little name for me,' she explained. 'Short for Priscilla, you know.'

'Of course.' Rosalind barely suppressed a smile.

'Now what was I saying?' the lady asked, having misplaced the somewhat tenuous thread of her thoughts.

'You were telling us what your husband used to say to you,' Julian informed her helpfully.

'Oh yes!' She paused, apparently attempting to recapture the stray bit of memory. 'He used to say, "Scilly, you'll never find another sapskull like me. I'll wager my life upon it"!'

'And you never have!' St George agreed, almost oversetting Rosalind with his air of mock gravity which was quite lost upon his poor cousin.

'Indeed not,' she agreed, her eyes misting suspiciously. 'Not that Mr Plummer wasn't a trial at times! But what man isn't?'

'You'll have no argument from me on that head,' Rosalind told her.

'And now, my beautiful dragon,' St George said to Rosalind, 'it is our turn to make you acquainted with our own lodgings. If you will allow me to escort you?'

Politeness demanded her acquiescence, and for the next half-hour they were led around the lodge which was the occasional residence of Julian's absent uncle – he of the warning letter, of which his present tenants were in blessed ignorance, Rosalind thought with inward self-satisfaction.

The lodge was a fairly commodious residence, with five bedchambers, a small dining-room, a much larger drawing-room, in addition to kitchens and servants' quarters. There was a great deal of oak panelling and lurid paintings of hunting scenes on the walls. In the small study, the most remarkable feature was a rug made from the skin of a grizzly bear from the Americas, which a previous Marchmont had shot with his own musket.

'I should be afraid,' Cassandra told Julian, pressing rather too close to him in Rosalind's opinion, 'that it would come to life some night and eat me!'

'And what a delectable morsel you would make,' he quizzed.

'But I am sure that Julian would rescue you from such peril,' St George added.

'It looks as though it would collect a great deal of dust.' Cousin Scilly's practical comment shattered any lingering trace of the supernatural or romantic.

'A housemaid's nightmare,' Rosalind agreed.

'A sad decline indeed.' St George shook his head. 'From a ferocious beast in an untamed wilderness to a servant's chore in a staid English study.'

'Like Don Juan,' Rosalind quizzed him in turn. 'From a dashing young lover to a toothless old dotard, drooling over the ankles of an indifferent parlour maid.'

'There is not an ounce of romance in you, Miss Powell,' Julian objected.

'I fear you are right, Julian – Mr Marchmont—' Cassandra corrected herself quickly. But Julian would have none of it.

'No, no, Miss Woodford!' he corrected. 'I hope we are better friends than that. My Christian name is at your disposal, if I may be permitted to call you by yours.'

So, Rosalind thought grimly, another step was being taken towards an intimacy from which no good could come. They seemed to be propelled forward now by the impetus of their initial rash decision. Where would this end?

Dinner was a much grander affair than they had ever experienced at the abbey. The gentlemen, it seemed, had a French cook. With their deplorable lack of *savoir-vivre*, Rosalind and Cassandra scarcely knew what they ate. It was undeniably tasty, though the number of courses seemed excessive and they were forced to leave a considerable amount on their plates. The two men, more accustomed to such lavish fare, had no qualms about consuming the vast quantity of victuals, and Cousin Scilly had an equally healthy appetite.

Afterwards, they retired to the drawing-room. After a few awkward moments in which nobody – even the indefatigable Mrs Plummer – seemed to know what to say, Julian hit upon an idea which created a minor sensation.

'Mrs Plummer,' he enquired hopefully, 'do you play the pianoforte?'

'Yes indeed,' the lady replied eagerly. 'Would you like some music?'

'We might each take a turn, if you like,' Rosalind said. At least, she reasoned, that would spare her any tête-à-tête with St George – or rather, Richard.

'To be frank,' Julian confessed, 'I was thinking that you might be persuaded to play for us while we danced.'

For a moment the two girls were both struck silent. Mrs Plummer was not so fortunate.

'What a splendid idea!' she almost yodelled in her delight.

'Do you two gentlemen,' Rosalind enquired, 'intend to dance together for our delectation?'

'Of course not.' Julian was not amused by the suggestion. 'I will partner Cassandra, if she will permit, while you and Richard can dance together.'

'We do not dance.'

Julian's glance at Rosalind when she made this unprecedented pronouncement was a study in stupefaction. Clearly he had failed to anticipate this.

'But all young ladies dance!' he protested, unable to credit something so eccentric.

'Except our two young ladies,' St George corrected him, though he did not look at all surprised.

'We have been reared,' Rosalind informed them, 'on very strict Evangelical principles.'

Here was a seemingly insurmountable obstacle to the progress of the gentlemen's schemes.

'You feel, perhaps, that Hannah More would not approve?' he asked Rosalind, referring to the famous English writer and reformer.

'I am certain that she would find very little in your behaviour of which she could approve.'

'I own,' Cassandra said rather diffidently, 'that I have always wondered what it would be like to dance.'

'Cass!' Rosalind shook her head in despair. Her charge seemed determined to lower her guard at every opportunity, surrendering to the enemy before they had even engaged in battle.

'Well, it is the truth, Lindy!' Cassandra blushed a little, but stood her ground. 'But how can a blind person learn the steps? It seemed a waste of time to employ a dancing master when neither of us was ever likely to make use of his lessons.'

'Forgive me,' Julian stammered. 'I did not mean – that is, sometimes I forget—'

'I see no reason,' St George, frowning, cut in on this muddled speech, 'why Rosalind, at least, could not have been taught.'

Cassandra seemed much struck by this. 'You are right, sir,' she said. 'I never even thought of it before. How selfish of us to assume that because I could not dance, Lindy might not benefit from learning.'

'Nonsense!' Rosalind quickly dismissed this onslaught of self-reproach. 'I never expressed any such wish, nor do I now. What opportunity would there be for me to employ such a skill?'

'You have one now,' St George reminded her. 'However, I agree that it would not be proper for me to stand up with you while Miss Woodford is forced to abstain.'

'I can imagine the havoc I should create in a country dance,' Cassandra added, recovering her humour almost at once, 'bumping into all and sundry, and tripping over everyone's feet – including my own.'

'But what about the waltz?' Cousin Priscilla suggested. 'There is nothing difficult about that, since one is guided by one's partner.'

'My dear cousin,' St George said, almost overcome with delight at this evidence of unsuspected intellect, 'what an inspired notion – a stroke of pure genius.'

'The waltz!' Rosalind could barely control her shock. 'Never could we be persuaded to participate in such a scandalous activity. I understand that it is the most indecent dance.'

'Oh, my dear Miss Powell,' Cousin Priscilla hastened to correct her, 'I assure you it is no such thing. It is danced everywhere in London, I believe – even at Almack's.' This last word was spoken in the most reverent tones, as befitted any reference to the hallowed halls of London's most exclusive assembly rooms, where only the pick of the *ton* were permitted entry.

'That is no recommendation, in my opinion.'

'I am sure that you would have no difficulty learning it, Cassandra,' Julian said eagerly. 'There is no danger of you falling, you know, since you would have my arm about you the whole time.'

No further persuasion was needed on the young lady's part.

'Oh, do let us try, Lindy!' Her face glowed with such youthful high spirits and happy anticipation that Rosalind felt her resolve weakening in spite of herself.

'If you find it offensive, my dear dragon,' St George continued to quiz her, 'you need only say the word and we will cease our dissipated revels at once.'

'Very well,' she consented grudgingly. 'You shall have a lesson with Mr Marchmont.'

'Julian,' he corrected her, flashing a curiously boyish smile which she found hard to resist.

'But only if you will allow St George to instruct you as well,' Cassandra insisted. 'I do not wish to be the only one made to look a fool for my lack of social graces.'

'There seems to be a confederacy against me,' Rosalind complained. Inwardly, she admitted to herself that the thought of having Richard St George's arm about her was far more tempting than it should be.

'There is no hope of victory, I'm afraid,' St George warned her. 'One must simply submit as gracefully as possible. And, should Miss More require an explanation for such frivolous behaviour, one can always argue that dancing is excellent exercise for the body, good for the circulation of the blood and contributing to grace and balance. I really consider it superior to sea bathing, myself.'

'I yield,' Rosalind answered with irony, 'to your superior knowledge of both.'

'I thought you would.'

With that, he held out his arms. She moved hesitantly towards him. She wasn't afraid of him, but she was very much afraid of the way her heart was beating and the strange prickly sensation at the back of her neck. Even knowing what he was, she seemed to have no control over her body's response. He put his right arm around her waist and drew her almost against him. At his word, she placed her left hand on his shoulder while her right hand was clasped in his left.

He commanded Mrs Plummer to play a slow waltz. The strong three-quarter rhythm with its emphasis on the first beat of each bar had an almost mesmeric effect upon her. Or was it Richard's eyes looking down so intently into her own?

'Now,' he said, softly but firmly, 'you step like this.'

Out of the corner of her eye she could see Cassandra similarly engaged with Julian, who was all patience and delicacy. Oh, why could his affection not be real, instead of a hateful simulation?

Either Rosalind was a most precocious pupil, or Richard a fine teacher, but they were twirling about the room in unison in almost no time at all. Cassandra took rather longer to acquire the skill and to overcome the unquestioned difficulties caused by her condition. But, by great care and persistence on Julian's part and her own eagerness, she managed to do reasonably well.

The fields and trees were silver-gilt from the light of a full moon when they returned home more than an hour later. A misty rain had fallen only a few minutes before their departure, and the droplets glistened here and there in the moonlight, like fairy lights amongst the underbrush.

All this Rosalind described to Cassandra as they progressed. It was a valient but futile effort to postpone the rapturous reminiscence which must ensue.

'Was it not absolutely divine?' Cassandra asked her friend.

'Very pleasant.'

But Rosalind's tepid response would not do.

'Lindy, you are a fraud,' Cassandra complained. 'You enjoyed it quite as much as I did, but refuse to admit it.'

'Did I not just say that it was pleasant?' Rosalind was glad that the other girl could not see the heightened colour in her cheeks. 'What more do you require of me?'

'A little less reticence and self-possession.' Cassandra subsided on to the cushioned carriage seat and closed her eyes, an instinctive action bearing no relation to their sense. 'Even you must own that waltzing with a man is the most exhilarating and wonderful experience. I truly felt as if I were flying – that my feet were not even touching solid ground!'

How could Rosalind, in all honesty, deny what Cassandra said? She had never been to a ball, never been escorted by a gentleman on to the floor to take part in the dance. She had never been so close to a man's body before – unless it were the occasional affectionate embrace from her uncle, which was not at all the same thing, she had discovered. But circling the floor in the arms of a man who – at least so far as looks and address were concerned – was everything she had ever dreamed of in the days when she had dared to dream at all, was a pleasure which was unsurpassed in her admittedly limited experience.

If not precisely divine, as Cass had described it, her feelings had certainly been more than just mild enjoyment. There was something about the waltz which was definitely not conducive to rational thought, she decided. Perhaps it was the constant turning about which made one's heart beat so fast and produced a sensation of light-headedness. She knew not how else to explain what had just occurred. She could have sworn that St George had felt something more as well. The intensity of his gaze, the pressure of his hand clasping hers . . . but then, she supposed he must have danced with scores of young women and had probably charmed them just as easily. She might have felt like a princess in his arms, but he was no prince! It was no use to indulge in schoolgirl daydreams. Rosalind might be in danger of losing her heart, but Miss Powell was determined not to lose her head! It was Miss Powell who finally responded to Cassandra.

'It was not wise to indulge in such disreputable behaviour,' she said primly, using her best governess-to-pupil tone. 'We are allowing those two men to take far too many liberties, and we must end this charade before it is too late.'

When Cassandra replied to this, it almost overset Rosalind, for it was not the response of a young girl any longer but that of one woman to another – with a disconcertingly adult intuition.

'My dearest Lindy.' She leaned against her friend and felt for her hand. 'You must not be so afraid of loving someone.'

'Afraid!' The word was all the more annoying because of its aptness.

'I know it will probably end in sadness,' the girl beside her continued with stoic resignation, 'but I have felt more alive these past weeks than ever before in my life. Julian and St George may not have meant this for our good, but I would not change it for the world! They have given us memories which I think we will both treasure all our lives.'

To this, Rosalind could say nothing, but only reflect silently on the words of Pascal: that the heart has it reasons which Reason knows not of. In theory, she disagreed with Cassandra completely, but life is more than theory, and love is not so neat and tidy as to be limited by logic. They had always been close, though their dispositions were very different, but what they shared now knit them together more than ever, for it was the unity of two women who were embarking on the most perilous journey of all, where the value of the prize to be gained was equalled only by the price which might be paid in ultimate loss.

CHAPTER TWELVE

The trio at the lodge were curiously quiet the next morning. Each man had his respective nose buried in a book which seemed to absorb all his attention, so that conversation had ceased entirely. Mrs Plummer remained upstairs, apparently fatigued by the exertions of the previous evening. At length, though, she appeared at the door of the drawing-room. St George was the first to become aware of her presence. A strange prickling sensation peculiar to those who feel that they are being observed caused him to look up. There was his cousin, her plump figure filling the doorway, an indulgent smile upon her face as she glanced from one to the other.

It struck him suddenly that she would have made a fine mother. There was something maternal and nurturing about her. It was one of those ironies of life, however, that though she had given birth to three children, none of them had survived infancy.

The two gentlemen stood at once and bid her good day.

'What a delightful picture you both make.' She sailed forward and hove to at the first available berth: a carved mahogany chair which scarcely looked sufficiently sturdy to support her.

'Reading,' she asserted, 'is what finishes a man's mind.' If she was aware of the ambiguous nature of this remark, she did not show it, adding only, 'Mr Plummer read nothing but the London newspapers, now that I think on it. One may learn much about a man by what he reads. What books have captured your attentions so entirely?'

'I am reading *The Song of Solomon*.' Julian shook his head, as though unable to believe the words printed on the page before him. 'Listen to this, Richard: "Thy navel is like a round goblet, which wanteth not liquor: thy belly is like an heap of wheat set about with lilies. Thy two breasts are like two young roes that are twins".'

'Most unusual and arresting images,' St George commented after Julian's animated recital.

'I remember my dear husband's favourite verse from the Scriptures.' Cousin Priscilla's eyes became suspiciously moist at the memory. 'From the first book of Samuel, I believe: "Surely there had not been left unto Nabal by the morning light any that pisseth against the wall".'

Julian's chin dropped almost to his chest at this latest example of the crudity of ancient texts. He declared himself amazed that such things should be contained in Holy Writ. For his part, St George could not decide which he found more piquant: the quotation itself, or the fact that Cousin Priscilla had for once – at least, as far as he could discern – managed to put the words in their proper order. The late Mr Plummer must have quoted them frequently – whenever he was in his cups, no doubt. He might even have preached a fine sermon upon that particular text when the spirits moved him. His speech might have been somewhat slurred, but St George fancied he could imagine the fire in Mr Plummer's eyes. At least they must have been a burning red.

'And what, pray, are you reading, Cousin?'

'My poor book is not nearly so entertaining,' Richard confessed. Nevertheless, it was with an air of conscious superiority that he continued: 'I am reading Mr Wilberforce's celebrated work, *The Practical View of the Prevailing Religious System of Professed Christians in the Higher and Middle Classes of this Country Contrasted with Real Christianity*.'

'You are roasting us!' Julian's disbelief was too apparent. 'I have never heard of such a book.'

'I am not surprised.' His tone was somewhat sardonic. 'The title is not, perhaps, as memorable as Mr Sterne's *Sentimental Journey*, but this is well worth reading, if one is prepared to face without flinching the general hypocrisy and insensibility of oneself and one's countrymen.'

'I declare,' Mrs Plummer said, beaming upon them, 'I had expected you both to be reading the latest novels from town. But I suppose one must make allowances for two gentlemen in love.'

'In love!' Julian cried, as though she had just boxed his ears. St George, while not so astonished as his younger friend, was conscious that the smile which had tugged at the corners of his mouth had disappeared.

'Of course!' Cousin Priscilla, quite unaware of having said anything particularly momentous, continued gaily, 'Why, you and Miss Woodford are smelling of May and April as strongly as ever I saw two young persons. And I could not be happier for you both. She is an angel, and I think you will deal famously together.'

'But I believe,' St George said, with slow deliberation, 'that you said there were two gentlemen in love in this room.'

She laughed outright at this. 'You cannot fool me, Cousin! If a man looked at me the way you look at Miss Powell, I would be like to swoon.'

'And how does Miss Powell look at me?' he asked, even more deliberately.

'As if you were the Devil!' She nodded sagely. 'It is often the way with young women of strong feeling.'

'Is it?'

'Indeed yes. You just pop the question, and see if I am not right.'

'I think not.'

'There is no need to be afraid.' His cousin clearly misunderstood his words. 'She needs only a little encouragement, I assure you.'

'I fear you are mistaken, my dear Cousin.' His voice was solemn, almost menacing. 'I am not in love with Miss Powell.'

She did not seem at all discomfited by what others would have perceived as a none too polite set-down. Indeed, she smiled more broadly and chuckled softly. She clearly did not believe his protestations.

'Well,' she told him, 'I will not tease you, sir. But I take leave to keep my own opinion. I am not clever, but as they say, "when the moon is right, I know a handsaw from a hawk".'

Before he could respond to this, they were interrupted by the delivery of a note addressed to the three of them. Since they had not bothered to become acquainted with anyone else in the small neighbourhood, it could only come from the abbey. It was St George who picked it up and opened the sealed document, which was a charming invitation from Miss Woodford, asking them if they would care to dine at the abbey that evening.

The handwriting was clearly Miss Powell's, and the mocking

smile returned to his lips as he wondered how much coaxing it had taken Cassandra to persuade her to pen it.

Naturally they accepted the invitation, and at eight o'clock they arrived at the building which was becoming so familiar to them all. As it was the same company which they had been keeping for the past few weeks, there was no variation of scene and nothing profound in the conversation. The dinner was the plain but filling fare which they had become accustomed to in this house. It was a far cry from the London soirées, the gaming hells and boxing matches which were the usual haunts of the gentlemen; yet nobody seemed in danger of succumbing to the megrims.

For Mrs Plummer it was probably a more exciting social life than she was used to in her small cottage near the coast of Kent. She was in raptures over everything, could find fault with nothing, and generally determined to grasp whatever mite of pleasure came her way.

But even St George had to own to himself that he was not in the least bored and looked forward as eagerly as any to the time spent at the abbey. Tonight they played a short game of charades. Cassandra produced a tolerable one:

'While my first is the sky on a clear summer day,
And my second a sheath for a young lady's ankle,
The whole is oft thought to be much in the way
And, to eager young suitors, may rankle!

The answer was 'bluestocking,' which was perhaps all the more poignant since the young lady had never seen the sky by day or night.

St George himself could not resist the following:

'My first is to pull through muck and through mire
And my next the reverse of the phrase to be "off".
Yet the whole, if one meet her unquenchable fire,
Even St George himself would not scoff!'

It did not take Miss Powell long to discern that the two halves of the word in question were 'drag' and 'on'. The whole, of course, spelt 'dragon,' which drew a laugh from all concerned except the young lady at whom it was so clearly directed. Nonetheless, the evening passed remarkably swiftly. The room became increasingly warm and the three ladies plied their fans briskly.

'The moon,' Julian said at last, 'is full tonight. Shall we take a turn outside?'

'I should love to see your gardens by moonlight,' Cousin Priscilla cried, ever eager.

'A wonderful idea,' St George agreed.

'Let me but fetch two shawls for us,' Rosalind was quick to say. There was no need for one for Mrs Plummer, who already sported a thick wool scarf in a bright shade of blue quite at odds with the purple gown she wore.

Rosalind hastened upstairs to search for the necessary items. It was but a few minutes before she returned to the drawing-room, and yet upon her return she discovered only one member of their little party present.

'Where are the others?' she demanded, with a degree of apprehension quite disproportionate to the situation.

'They are gone on ahead into the gardens,' St George explained. 'Miss Woodford remembered that she had left a shawl on the chair over against the wall there.'

111

He gestured in the direction of a shadowed corner where Cassandra often liked to sit while Rosalind read to her. She now remembered that they had done so earlier, and that she had indeed been wearing a shawl at the time. Perhaps she was too eager to ascribe ignoble motives to the gentleman. Not all his actions must be calculated and cunning, she supposed.

'But they need not have left so quickly,' she complained. She felt the faintest tingle of apprehension down her back. The room seemed much darker and more intimate suddenly. She almost jumped when the gentleman moved towards her.

'They were eager for a little fresh air,' he said reasonably. 'It is rather close in here, is it not?'

'Yes.'

'And you need not fear for the reputation of your charge,' he added, that mocking smile playing at the corners of his lips. 'Mrs Plummer is with them. And I assured them that I was perfectly content to wait here for you.'

'Thank you, sir.' The conventional response did not come easily.

He held out his hand and took one of the shawls from her, depositing it on a nearby sofa. Then, turning back towards her, he offered his arm. She felt obliged to accept it.

'Shall we follow their example?'

The garden by moonlight was a strange, unearthly landscape. Whatever was not hidden in soft folds of darkness seemed starkly etched in steel. The paths were of polished stones, the roses silver gilt and dew-encrusted in beds of black velvet. The statues were weird wraiths rising out of the foliage.

Rosalind followed St George into this enchanted yet oddly forbidding world, hoping that they would soon catch sight of the trio who had gone on ahead. There was no sign of them, however, and Rosalind soon grew impatient.

'Are you certain that they came this way?'

'No,' he answered, not a whit perturbed. 'They went in the opposite direction.'

'Then why have you brought me here?' she snapped, quite out of patience.

'Because I wanted to be alone with you.'

She caught her breath, wondering if she could have heard him correctly. There was an air of deliberation about him tonight. She felt that the mask he had been wearing was slipping and she was about to find out what was behind it.

'Why,' she enquired between clenched teeth, 'should you wish to be alone with me, sir?'

'Can you not guess?' The note of sardonic humour in his voice made her uneasy, but she refused to be intimidated.

'I presume your intentions to be everything of the most dishonourable.'

They were standing beneath a vine-covered arbour, the moonlight filtering through in patches of quivering light and shade. Between them was an armillary sphere which offered little in the way of protection against him.

'How well you understand me, my dear dragon.' He moved to the right and so did she, circling about the armillary. 'I knew that subterfuge would be useless with you.'

'You are playing a deep game,' she said, wondering how far away the others were, and whether they would hear her if she screamed. 'But you cannot fool me. I am well aware of your – your machinations.'

'What do you suppose the others would think,' he asked, completely ignoring her words, 'if they were to find you in my arms, being thoroughly kissed?'

'There is little likelihood of such an eventuality,' she flung at him. But in the semi-gloom she had underestimated how near he was, for suddenly his hand shot out around the edge of the armillary and grasped her own hand with punishing force.

'On the contrary.' He sounded as though he were discussing the weather. 'If they come upon us a minute from now, that is precisely what they will see.'

While he spoke, he was moving around until he stood directly before her. A stray shaft of moonlight illumined his face for a brief moment. There was a dark, dangerous glitter in his eyes.

'Why are you doing this?' She was amazed by the steadiness of her own voice. Her knees felt about as steady as a blanc-mange.

'Because I am a man.' He pulled her against him, her soft breasts against his rock-hard chest, her face looking up into his. 'And you, my lovely Rosalind, are the most beautiful and desirable woman I have ever known.'

She should have screamed. She should at least have swooned. There could be no doubt that he meant what he said, and everything she had been taught cried out that it was sinful and wrong. Unfortunately, her body was sending a very different message to her very confused mind. Being so near to him, hearing his voice grow husky with passion, something stirred inside of her that she had never before imagined. So, when he lowered his mouth to hers, she behaved in exactly the opposite manner from what she should have. When his tongue parted her lips, she was already beyond resistance; when his hold tightened and that first kiss was repeated with renewed excitement and pleasure, she matched his desire with her own. His hands caressed her and her arms slid around his neck. She buried her fingers in his thick dark hair, holding his mouth against her own while she stroked his neck.

For the merest instant he raised his head and their glances met, fire stoking fire. She could scarcely breathe.

'Shall I stop now?' he asked her, his own breathing ragged, as if he had just been running.

'No,' she whispered.

He needed no further encouragement. With a groan half of victory and half of animal hunger, he pressed his mouth to hers again. She was out of her senses with his kisses, his touch. It did not even matter that he did not care for her. All that mattered was this moment, and the unbearable pleasure of their shared desire.

How long this lasted, or what the end would have been, Rosalind did not know. As if from a long distance away, she vaguely heard a sound – shrill, piercing, ripping through the veil of passion with the sharp thrust of grim reality.

'Hallooo! St George! Miss Powell! Where are you?'

With a strength born of desperation, Rosalind pushed herself away from him. He looked down at her, appearing dazed and dishevelled in the moonlight.

'If we are silent,' he whispered at last, 'she may go away.'

'Here we are, Mrs Plummer!' Rosalind called out. She was but too tempted to be silent. The taste of him was still on her tongue, more sweet than she could ever have dreamed. But she knew it to be only wormwood.

He released her with such abruptness that she nearly fell. But his right hand remained around her left wrist. With a start, she realized that he was trembling. They both were. For her, it was hardly surprising, since her world had just been turned thoroughly upside down.

'Coward!' he chided her, beginning to regain his own composure.

' "Conscience doth make cowards of us all",' she quoted, attempting a lighter tone.

'Except for those of us fortunate enough not to possess a conscience.'

'I am not one of the fortunate few.'

'You cannot deny that you were tempted.'

'I am human.' She swallowed. 'I was weak. But it will not happen again.'

' "Some rise by sin",' he quipped, ' "and some by virtue fall".'

Rosalind pulled her arm from his grasp and tried to tidy her hair and her gown. Her shawl had fallen to the ground and Richard bent to retrieve it.

'Ah! There you are.' Cousin Priscilla descended upon them. 'We have been looking for you this age. Cassandra was growing quite worried.'

'Have you left her alone with Julian?' Rosalind was near hysteria, wondering whether the young girl was being treated to the same kind of sauce that she had just been served.

'They are right behind me,' Mrs Plummer reassured her, and indeed at that moment the other two appeared out of the darkness.

Richard, meanwhile, placed Rosalind's shawl carefully about her shoulders, deliberately trailing a finger along the nape of her neck as he did so. She stepped away at once.

'We were having such a delightful conversation,' he told the others, 'that we quite forgot the time.'

'What was it that engrossed you so completely?' Julian raised an eyebrow, as if well aware of the nature of their *discussion*.

'We were speaking of temptation – and of conscience.'

'Forgive me,' Rosalind told Cassandra, eager to turn the subject. 'I did not mean to alarm you.'

'It is quite all right.' Cass hugged her friend. 'It was an

inspired idea of Julian's, was it not?'

'Inspired,' Rosalind repeated, barely suppressing a shudder at how near to ruin she had come because of it.

'Of course,' Cassandra continued, with her usual self-deprecating wit, 'day and night are the same to me.'

'But one can feel the difference in the night air,' Julian reminded her. 'The moon's light is more gentle, the breeze caresses rather than invigorates.'

Cassandra had to agree with this. 'Even the smells and sounds of the night are more subtle. There is a stillness, as though the world itself were resting.'

Rosalind felt as though she herself would never rest again. She could hardly wait for their guests to be gone. It was growing late, however, and her torment was short-lived. The party from the lodge soon departed. Rosalind knew that Cassandra would want to have a long coze with her, but she excused herself at once with the plea of being over-fatigued. Cass cocked her head to the side like an inquisitive bird. But if she doubted her friend's veracity, she did not press the matter. Perhaps she understood something of the feelings inside the older girl's breast – which was more than Rosalind herself could claim.

Shutting the door of her bedchamber firmly behind her, Rosalind went over to the small writing-desk in the far corner and sat down. With her elbow on the desktop, she leaned over and rested her forehead on her open palm. She felt ill. She felt wonderful. She felt changed in some indefinable way, and almost feared to face a mirror lest she not recognize her own countenance. What was she to do? She had worried so much that Cassandra might not come out of this adventure heart-whole. It had not really occurred to her that her own heart might be at risk – until now, when she feared it was already too late.

Sitting up straight and squaring her shoulders, she looked at the familiar, comforting objects on the desk: a small knife, some sealing wax, a fresh quill and an inkwell. It came to her then that she must do now what she should have done from the very first. Her only regret was that she had delayed for so long.

CHAPTER THIRTEEN

Mrs Plummer and the two men called at the abbey the next day. Cassandra and Welly greeted them enthusiastically. Of Miss Powell, however, there was no sign. Miss Woodford apologized for the absence of her companion, explaining that 'poor dear Lindy' was laid up in bed with a headache.

St George would have wagered that Rosalind had been perfectly well until she heard them arriving at the front door. Under other circumstances, he might have quizzed Cassandra upon this subject, but this time he refrained. In truth, he was conscious of a sensation of relief at the news.

Last night had revealed something of Miss Powell's feelings for him. More importantly, however, they had shown him something of *his* feelings for *her*, which was far more disturbing. To begin with, everything had gone just as he planned: he had manoeuvred her into the garden with the skill of an old campaigner. He had handled her just as he ought, he judged: his candour had disconcerted her and caused her to let down her guard. Then he had kissed her – and his plan had flown out of the window.

Never had he encountered such a bewitching combination of innocence and passion. Not since his salad days had he known such ardour within himself. He lost all sense of time, of place, of the reason for his pursuit of her. Holding her in his arms, tasting the incomparable sweetness of her lips, he was aware only of his own growing desire. Not the most beautiful of his mistresses had ever moved him so. Normally, he was in complete control of his emotions. His conquests had been mere trophies, which ceased to interest him as soon as they were won. But there in the abbey garden, he had felt his self-control slipping away like a boat cut loose from its moorings in a hurricane. Indeed, there had been a tempest within him which raged with a fury beyond all he had ever experienced.

Perhaps it was best that he did not see Rosalind Powell again. Something in his mind flashed like a light warning sailors of a shoal ahead. There was more danger in this enterprise than he had at first imagined. With persistence, he might yet win that wager. Whatever else was true, he knew that he had stirred Rosalind Powell's desire as much as she aroused his. On the other hand, he could afford the loss of a thousand pounds. It was a mere trifle compared to – to what? What did he stand to lose if he continued with this madness? His soul? He had quite forgotten that he possessed such a thing. He did not wish to be reminded of it now.

'I do hope,' Cousin Priscilla's voice interrupted his musings, 'that Miss Powell is not very ill. I knew a lady who went to head with a grievous bedache, and was dead within the hour.'

'Miss Powell is perfectly healthy, I am sure.' Richard frowned, more irritated than ever at his cousin's ill-considered bibble-babble. 'Perhaps she stayed awake too late last night.'

'I fear that we have infected you both with our wicked London ways,' Julian quizzed Cassandra. 'Waltzes and moonlight walks . . . such dissipation!'

'Dear Julian!' Nobody could mistake the warmth and sincerity in the lady's voice. 'You have no notion how much knowing you both has meant to Lindy and me. These weeks have been some of the happiest and gayest we have ever spent, and I am sure that neither of us will ever forget them – or you.'

'You do not think, then, that we have caused the exhaustion of the long-suffering Miss Powell?' It was St George's turn to quiz her now.

'She has an excellent constitution,' Cassandra asserted. 'I have no doubt that she will be up and about by tomorrow.'

'Perhaps even sooner,' he suggested.

'Do you think she might be persuaded to join us for another outing?' Cousin Priscilla enquired. 'Julian and I have put our heads together and come up with the most delightful scheme.'

'Oh!' Cassandra cried. 'Do tell me about it.'

'But be warned,' St George intervened, 'it is most unlikely that the redoubtable Miss Powell will approve.'

'Nonsense!' Cassandra contradicted him with a laugh. 'You may call her a dragon, sir, but I assure you the warmest thing about Lindy is her heart. Like Welly here, her bark is much more alarming than her bite.'

'Nevertheless, I think you will find it hard to persuade her this time.'

Cassandra soon discovered that St George had not been mistaken in his prediction. Presented with the proposed plan, Rosalind flatly refused to have anything to do with it.

'But think, Lindy! If you do not go, how can I?'

'Really, Cass, I think it best if you do not go either.'

'Do not be so stuffy.' Cassandra knew that she was pouting, but she had recourse to all her weapons in this skirmish. 'Cousin Priscilla says that the lake – or pond – is just over an acre in size and a lovely spot for a picnic.'

'Suppose one of us happened to fall in?' Rosalind was determined, it seemed, to view everything in the most gloomy light possible. 'Neither of us can swim. And, in case you have forgotten the fact, you happen to be blind.'

'I assure you, it is something I never forget.'

Cassandra had long ago determined not to dwell on her condition. Remembering that 'what cannot be cured must be endured', she accepted her lot and never indulged in useless self-pity. Perhaps it was not quite fair to Rosalind to fling this spurious plea for sympathy at her. But what else could she do? How else was she to acquire her consent? What did it matter if her tactics were less than honest, so long as they were effective?

'Forgive me, Cass.' The remorseful response was instantaneous. 'How unfeeling of me.'

Cassandra felt her friend's affectionate and apologetic embrace. It occurred to her that Rosalind had been behaving strangely for several days. It was as if the older woman were avoiding her company. They had not even had an opportunity to discuss the evening party two days previously.

'Do not ask me to go on this picnic, dearest,' Rosalind pleaded. 'I do not think my nerves will stand it.'

'I have never known you to be nervous before.' Cassandra was taken aback. This was a new Rosalind, one with whom she was not yet acquainted. 'What happened between you – and Richard in the garden the other evening?'

Rosalind drew away abruptly. 'Why do you ask me such a question?'

'It is obvious that something happened.' She did not mince matters. 'You have been most elusive since then, and your convenient headache today was quite unconvincing. I think you must go on this picnic, if only by way of apology to Julian and Cousin Priscilla.'

'I did not mean – you do not understand.' The normally

fluent Miss Powell was plainly disconcerted.

'Did St George – did Richard . . . did he . . . um . . . *ravish* you that night?'

Cassandra waited with bated breath for the answer to this indelicate question. She was not disappointed.

'No!' Rosalind cried emphatically, then promptly spoilt this by adding, 'Perhaps . . . yes . . . I don't know.'

'Well, I have never been ravished by a man.' Cassandra's brow furrowed in an effort of concentration. 'But I should think I would know if I had.'

'He kissed me. That is all.'

'How wonderful!' Cassandra was ecstatic at this news.

'Wonderful!' Rosalind repeated, her voice clearly expressing that this was not the word she would have used to describe it.

'I am green with envy and feel quite ill-used,' Cassandra complained. 'Julian has never done more than hold my hand! He treats me with a degree of respect almost bordering on reverence – and, frankly, it is becoming unbearably vexatious.'

'Cassandra!' Rosalind's tone was one of severe reproof.

'Don't pretend to be shocked, Lindy.' Cassandra was growing impatient. 'I would have kissed Julian myself, only I am doubtful of finding his lips. I should probably end up kissing his nose instead. I have even considered asking him to kiss me, but have not the courage.'

'You sound as wanton as – as—'

'Aholah and Aholibah?' Cassandra finished, recalling the two 'sisters' in Ezekiel's parable.

'Perhaps not so bad as that.'

'Are we harlots, do you think?'

'No!'

'You are not lusting after St George, like the Assyrians and Chaldeans, then?' Cassandra was comically earnest. 'Perhaps I am like Aholibah, the younger sister . . . .'

'Don't be absurd!' Rosalind admonished her, glad that Cassandra could not see the deep colour in her face as she remembered how she had responded to St George. 'We are not wanton women.'

'Perhaps not.' Cassandra caught delicate lips between her teeth. 'But this is the closest to a real romance that I am ever likely to come, Lindy, and I do not want to live my life without knowing what it is like to be kissed – properly kissed – by a young man.'

'Oh, Cass!' There was a distinct tremor to her friend's voice now, and Cassandra was astonished to realize that she was on the point of tears. This was quite unprecedented in the ruthlessly unsentimental Rosalind Powell.

'If your reaction to St George's kiss is any indication,' Cassandra continued more gently, but with unflagging determination, 'it must have been something quite out of the common way.'

'Oh, it was.'

Then the whole story came tumbling from Rosalind's lips. Cassandra, listening in something like awe, wondered how she could have kept it to herself even for these two interminable days. That her feelings for the man were stronger than anything she had ever known was apparent. For the first time, Cassandra began to question the wisdom of allowing themselves to become embroiled in the dishonourable scheme which Julian's uncle had disclosed. It had seemed like a wonderful adventure, in which she had been prepared to risk her own heart: never had it occurred to her that she might be risking Rosalind's as well. Rosalind was so strong-willed, so straitlaced. How could she have imagined such an outcome?

'Dearest Lindy.' She reached out and felt for the other girl's arm, threading hers through it. 'One thing you must not do is to let him see that he has any power over you. You must accompany us on this picnic, if only to prove this to him.'

'You are right.' She took a deep breath, and Cassandra could feel her body become less rigid as she began to reclaim her composure.

'Besides, you shall not be alone with him again.' With a quick, reassuring hug, she added, 'I shall be there, and so will Julian and Mrs Plummer. There will be no opportunity for St George to compromise you in any way.'

CHAPTER FOURTEEN

The day of the picnic dawned clear and warm. It was a day made to be out of doors. Surveying her reflection in the glass above her small dressing-table, Rosalind tried to tell herself that she was confident and unafraid. She was in good looks, she knew. Her muslin dress was the colour of spring daffodils, with a white spencer jacket embroidered over with flowers. A wide-brimmed bonnet of chipped straw with yellow and white ribbons completed her ensemble.

At least she looked carefree and unconcerned. But how great an actress would she prove to be? It would not be easy to face Richard St George again after that memorable scene in the abbey garden. She had never lacked courage, but she had never encountered an opponent so perilous. He had overcome her in their last engagement. Having lost that battle so completely, was there any hope of recovery? Could she still win the war?

Standing beside Cassandra, she watched Sir Jasper's sturdy but rather dated landau draw near, its team of dappled horses perfectly paced, with St George himself handling the ribbons. Amid the chorus of greetings, she managed a polite nod in his direction as they settled in. Seated beside Mrs Plummer at the rear of the vehicle, Rosalind was grateful that the only thing she could see of the man was his back as he drove with the practised ease to be expected of a member of the Four Horse Club.

The drive was uneventful, with Priscilla chattering away in her sometimes scarcely intelligible phrases while Cassandra and Julian carried on a low-toned conversation of their own behind St George's back. They skirted the lodge proper, drawing up some distance behind it on a grassy expanse which led up to the very edge of the pond, which was almost a small lake.

'Here we are!' Julian announced, descending eagerly.

'I'll wager it is a most romantic spot.' Cassandra took his hand and stepped down on to the grass.

Rosalind was not sure that she would have described it as romantic. It should have been set in a clearing in the midst of a lush green forest, with swans gliding over the rippling surface of the water. A gaggle of geese did indeed waddle up out of the water on the other side and disappear amongst the dense reeds springing up around much of the perimeter, but they were more rustic than romantic. There was a stand of larches on the western edge of the pond. Nearer than this was a very small jetty with a weathered dinghy moored to it.

Immediately before them was their picnic. The servants had already arranged everything and could be seen retreating towards the lodge as they approached. Several coverlets were spread out on the grass under a canvas canopy which looked surprisingly sturdy. There were five baskets which no doubt contained their luncheon. Everything had obviously been care-fully planned, and Rosalind was forced to admit that it all looked very festive and inviting.

127

Surveying this with interest, Rosalind scarcely noticed that Mrs Plummer had already exited the carriage.

'If you will, ma'am,' St George's voice interrupted her silent perusal.

She realized that he was waiting to hand her down from the carriage. Swallowing the lump of anxiety which had suddenly risen to her throat, she placed her hand in his and allowed him to assist her to descend. For a moment she met his gaze, only to turn away in dismay. The sun might be shining, but the unconcealed desire in his eyes seemed more appropriate to the moonlight. Despite her best resolution, she felt her body's instant response and her heart pounded uncontrollably in her breast.

'Did I not say that it was a perfect spot?' Mrs Plummer asked rhetorically. 'It reminds me of the Twenty-third Psalm: "He leadeth me beside still pastures; He maketh me to lie down in green waters; He prepareth an enemy for me in the presence of my table . . .".'

Her absurd misquotation was like a bucket of cold water on the hot flush of passion. Rosalind could see Cassandra bite her lips in an effort to control her mirth, while Julian gave a suspicious cough and St George looked away determinedly.

They settled down in their Elysian field to gorge themselves on a sumptuous repast. There were thick slices of freshly baked bread and a dish of creamy yellow butter, cold sliced ham, a variety of fresh fruit, jams, jellies and sauces, a kind of salad made with peeled and sliced potato and fresh vegetables. The gentlemen shared from a bottle of wine and there was a mild negus to refresh the ladies.

Following this feast, a general lassitude descended upon them. Reclining in the shade, there seemed little inclination for speech. Even the indefatigable Mrs Plummer was affected, falling into a comfortable doze on a plump silk cushion. It must have been a quarter of an hour before Julian stirred himself.

'I thought I spied a couple of oars in that boat by the shore there. I am sure nobody would mind if we borrowed it for an hour or so.' He directed this observation primarily towards Miss Woodford. 'What do you say, Cassandra? Shall we have a try?'

'Do you mean to take me rowing?' Her tone left no doubt that her answer would be 'yes'.

'That is most unwise.' Rosalind could not sanction such a foolish scheme.

'I will take the greatest care of her,' Julian urged, looking so much like a hopeful schoolboy that she felt her disapproval waver.

'Perhaps if we were to accompany you . . . .'

'The boat is only large enough to accommodate two, I'm afraid,' St George said. 'But if you would like to have a turn, I would be happy to take you out when Julian and Cassandra come back.'

'That is not necessary, sir.'

She might as well have spoken to the wind, for all the effect it produced. Perhaps her protestations were too feeble, for she found herself following the other three across the grass to the small boat. In a very few minutes, Julian and Cassandra were deposited in the vessel. They were joined by Welly, who had followed them and promptly jumped in behind his mistress, settling on her lap and apparently looking forward to a 'sea voyage'. St George pushed them away from the little wooden jetty.

'How delightful!' Cassandra cried, as Julian took the oars and they slipped away across the water. After that, there was little noise but the occasional call of a thrush and the muted laughter which drifted from the boat as they made their way around the pond.

The moment Rosalind had been dreading was now upon her. She was alone with the man whom she feared as much as she desired.

'I should return to Mrs Plummer,' she said, turning toward their shaded bower.

'I do not think she would appreciate you disturbing her rest, Rosalind.'

He had the impertinence to use her name! Then, considering their last encounter, perhaps he felt that he had earned that right.

'I have no intention of disturbing her.' She opened her sunshade with a snap. 'I merely thought that I might lie down and rest myself.'

'You need not run away from me, sweetheart,' he quizzed her. 'Even I would not dare to kiss you in full view of the others.'

'Kindly refrain from referring to me in such terms.' Her back stiffened and she met his laughing gaze with one of icy anger. 'And if you should choose to kiss me, the only one who would be able to see anything at the moment would be Julian – and I don't think that he would be likely to rescue me!'

'True.' He actually had the effrontery to smile. 'Indeed, he might well assume that you had no wish to be rescued.'

'You are a devil!' she spat at him, knowing that his remark had been too near the truth.

Suddenly the rather satiric look which he usually wore disappeared. His smile became more warm, more genuine.

'Let us call a truce, my dear dragon,' he said. 'Tempted as I am, if you will but consent to sit beside me and watch those two lovebirds on the pond, I promise to behave myself with the dullest of decorum. And if I should forget my good intentions,' he added wickedly, 'you could always scream as loudly as you can. I am sure that you would receive succour at once.'

So saying, he removed his jacket and laid it upon the grass indicating that she should seat herself. This exaggerated courtesy made it difficult for her not to return his smile: difficult, but not impossible. With a wooden countenance, she sat down and watched him lower himself beside her. For several minutes they sat in silence. She looked steadfastly forward at the water, though she was aware that he was observing her intently. This was too much to be borne.

'How did your cousin come to join you here?' she asked at length, casting about for some safe topic of conversation.

'She is here to lend us countenance,' he said, without dissimulation. 'I had to find someone amongst my numerous relations who was respectable enough that you would not object to her as a chaperone.'

'She seems most amiable and amusing.' She would not give him the pleasure of discomposing her today!

'A pleasant pea-goose,' he agreed. 'Just what I needed, in fact: the quintessential poor relation whose circumstances are so straitened that she can scarcely afford to refuse my invitation.'

'Yes,' she said, and could not quite keep the note of bitterness from her voice. 'We poor relations can be most useful at times.'

For once she had the pleasure of seeing *him* disconcerted.

'Forgive me,' he said, clearly angry with himself for his *faux pas*. 'I did not mean—'

'You need not apologize,' she interrupted. 'At least I am treated better by my uncle and cousin than Mrs Plummer must have been treated by her perpetually castaway husband.'

'With no fortune and no beauty,' St George said, 'I suppose she considered herself fortunate to have received an offer from that gentleman – or indeed, from any gentleman.'

'That is the sort of good fortune without which I am quite content.'

'So how did you come to live with Mr Woodford and your cousin?'

He seemed genuinely interested, and Rosalind found herself saying more than she had ever said to anyone else. Of course, there had never really been anyone to discuss such matters with. Neither Cassandra nor Uncle Frederick would have appreciated her thoughts on such a subject.

Her mother was a clergyman's daughter and her father a captain in the Shropshire militia. They had married young and quickly produced five children, of whom Rosalind was the fourth. Mrs Powell and two of her offspring had been carried off in an epidemic of influenza, and the good captain promptly farmed out his children to his brother and his wife, who were childless. Even so, they found the care and support of three children more of a burden than they had anticipated. So when Mr Woodford – the half brother of the children's deceased mother – suggested that he might be willing to take one of the girls, they were eager to send Rosalind off to live with him and his daughter. That left them with only two brats to care for. The elder, a boy named Edward, was soon sent to sea to serve on His Majesty's ship, *Olympia*. Sophie, the youngest child, remained at home.

At first, Rosalind had written regularly to all of them. Edward attempted a few badly spelled missives; Sophie, a year younger than Rosalind, kept up a correspondence for some time. Gradually, however, the letters grew less frequent and eventually ceased altogether. Sophie was now a wife and mother herself. Edward, she understood, was an able lieutenant with not unfounded hopes for promotion soon to captain. Her aunt was become a chronic invalid whose care had fallen upon her husband. Of her father, Rosalind had heard nothing for several years. Whether he were alive or dead, she knew not, and assumed, from his want of all communication, that he neither knew nor cared how she got on.

'At least,' St George said gently, when she finished her recital, 'you have been placed in an enviable position, compared to your siblings. Neither your sister nor brother is likely to have had the education you have received nor the elegant accommodations which you are afforded at the abbey.'

'True,' she nodded, dispelling her momentary gloom. 'I hope that I am not guilty of ingratitude towards my uncle. And Cassandra is more like a younger sister to me than Sophia is ever likely to be. They have both been more kind to me than I have deserved.'

To her surprise, he leaned over, took her hand in his and raised it to his lips.

'That,' he said emphatically, 'I refuse to believe!'

Once again her heart began to beat uncomfortably. The warmth in his eyes, the pressure of his hand, could so easily stir up her emotions! She could not look away, could not withdraw her fingers from his grasp.

'Lindy!' a high-pitched, youthful voice called out. 'You must take a turn on the water. It is the most heavenly feeling.'

Cassandra and Julian had returned to the little jetty. With a start, Rosalind drew back from Richard, who got up at once and stooped to help her stand. Then they both walked the few paces down to the pond and helped Julian to lift Cassandra out on to the bank. Welly scampered off into the grass, as though relieved to be on solid ground once more.

'Shall we take a turn now, Miss Powell?' St George asked

Rosalind with exaggerated formality.

'I do not know if—'

'Well, I do know!'

Cassandra would brook no argument, so Rosalind reluctantly allowed herself to be assisted into the tiny vessel, which rocked alarmingly until she was seated in the centre of the wooden plank which served as a seat.

A sudden mood of rebelliousness overcame her. After all, it could not be long before this idyll – sham though it might be – would come to an end. She would probably never see this man again, never glide across a lake in the company of a tall, dark, handsome Corinthian. This was all she would ever know of romance, so why should she not make the most of what crumbs were offered her? In a few days, it would all be no more than a memory.

'What of your own childhood, sir?' she asked, with some boldness, as he dipped the oars in the water and they drew away from the bank towards the centre of the pond.

He smiled that breath-stealing smile again. 'I will tell you something of myself, if you will agree to call me Richard.'

'Very well, Richard.'

'Unlike you, Rosalind,' he began, appearing very much at ease, 'I am the sole child of my poor parents.'

'How tragic,' she remarked, not fooled by his mock-mournful tone.

'My father was an MP, and much too busy with weighty matters to be bothered with the upbringing of his son and heir.'

'And your mother?'

'My mother . . .' There was a wry twist of his lips as he mentally exhumed the memories from wherever he had buried them. 'My mother was a toast of the *ton* in her youth, and is even now a bosom bow of Mrs Drummond Burrell. Both my parents were very well-connected, but she came of quite an illustrious family, and numbers more than one peer among her closest relations.'

'And are you close to your mother?' she could not resist asking.

'As close as I was to my father,' he replied with a self-deprecating shrug. 'She would often kiss my cheek on her way to a ball or ridotto. I remember the scent she used.' He seemed surprised at that, as if it had not occurred to him before. 'A faint trace of lavender, I think.'

'And where are your parents now?'

'My father shuffled off this mortal coil some years ago. My mother married again, and is now Lady Bettisham. I see her very seldom – though quite as often as either of us would wish.'

He treated the matter lightly, but Rosalind felt that she had seldom heard so sad a tale. She had often wished for her family, but it seemed that having family was no guarantee of being loved or valued. She tried to picture St George as a child. Pampered and privileged he might have been, but the most important needs of children had been wanting. Poor little boy!

She knew that he had served honourably in the army, though he had been in India at the time of Waterloo. When questioned about this, however, he was more reticent.

'My time in India is one which I prefer to forget.'

'The memories are so unpleasant?' She was surprised. Most men, she thought, would have been glad to regale her with exaggerated tales of their heroic exploits.

'Many of my comrades were enchanted with India.' He let the oars drop and the boat drifted silently. 'I was not so impressed, unfortunately.'

'Is it not a beautiful country?'

'Very lovely – once you look past the appalling customs like *suttee* and the cruel injustices wrought by the Law of Karma, which are not merely commonplace but often institutionalized.'

'Our own country,' she ventured, 'has its share of cruel customs as well.'

'Believe me, ma'am,' he said grimly, 'they pale in comparison with what I have witnessed out there. If anything could make me appreciate England, my time in India did so.'

She did not know what to say to this, and for some time there was silence between them. Only the faint sound of the oars pushing them onward disturbed the stillness. He had spoken with real feeling, albeit some bitterness. She was trying desperately to think of something else which they might discuss without incident, when a sudden sound captured her attention.

Turning her head, she spied three young boys emerging from the stand of trees towards which the boat was drifting. They were all about the same age: ten or eleven years old, she would guess. One of the them clutched a small sack of rough worsted fabric. It was from this sack that the sound was emerging in a shrill wail. At first Rosalind had thought it was a baby's cry. She was, after all, not much accustomed to children. But it quickly became apparent that what was contained in the sack was almost surely feline in nature.

'What are you doing there?' she cried out, craning her neck to see. 'Let that animal go at once!'

The trio was startled into immobility. They stared at the two occupants of the boat.

'What's it to yer?' the one with the sack shouted back. 'We ain't breakin' any law.'

'There *should* be a law,' she muttered under her breath.

Then, before she could answer them, St George called out in his much more authoritative voice:

'Let that animal go at once, or I shall come ashore and thrash every last one of you!'

'You and who else?' one of the lads jeered.

Rosalind was so angry that she forgot where she was. Rising from her seat, she opened her mouth and said, 'If you do—'

Alas, she was able to say no more. Though normally sure-footed, she was unused to maritime vessels. One minute she stood erect and ferocious; the next instant, she pitched backward into the pond with a great splash.

Julian, meanwhile, had been watching this spectacle, while Cassandra listened intently. Even Mrs Plummer had roused herself and looked out at the scene being enacted on the water.

'Rosalind!' Cassandra was near hysteria. She could only hear the commotion before her, but what was happening remained a mystery. 'St George, help her! She cannot swim!'

She had barely enough time to enunciate his name before St George was over the side and in the water with Rosalind. He dived down and brought her up quickly, enjoining her not to struggle. She obeyed him at once, and he managed to haul her to the side of the boat with surprisingly little effort.

Sputtering and gasping, her first words were, 'I must look an absolute fright!'

He threw back his head and laughed aloud, as much from relief as anything else. 'Only a woman would think of such a thing at a time like this,' he said, when he was able to control his mirth.

Cassandra, meanwhile, was so distrait that she stumbled forward and promptly tumbled down the gentle slope of the bank and landed in the shallows of the pond, creating her own aquatic spectacle. Julian, directly behind her, fished her out almost before she had time to realize that she was wet.

'Oh dear!' Cousin Priscilla, bouncing toward them with eyes now very wide open, could scarcely credit what had happened. 'Are you all well? Are you drowned? My nerves are quite overset. Such a picnic to our end!'

Clinging to the side of the boat, Rosalind suddenly recollected the cause of this fantastic imbroglio.

'Where are those oafs?' she demanded. 'Have they let the cat out of the bag?'

As if in response, there came a great yowl from the bank. The boys were nowhere to be seen, but their sack, wriggling and squirming, rested near the water's edge.

'Shall we complete our mission of mercy?' St George asked.

'Cassandra!' Rosalind called, glancing over her shoulder, belatedly enquiring after her young friend's fate.

'I am here, Lindy!' a cheerful voice answered. 'Julian has saved me from a watery grave.'

While she spoke, St George swam around to the stern of the dinghy and began to push it towards the bank. A moment later, Rosalind's feet touched the muddy bottom and she let go of the boat and waded towards the spot where the poor creature lay captive. A strong hold on her arm made her aware that Richard had caught up with her. He placed his arm around her – in the capacity of a helper rather than a lover this time – and assisted her on to solid ground. The little fiends had tied a sturdy knot to hold their victim, and it took almost a minute for St George to untangle it.

After all their efforts, they looked down at the ball of fur before them. This was no cat: it was a kitten, perhaps five or six weeks old. It could fit in the palm of his hand, he thought. As soon as it was released, it ceased to cry. Neither did it run away in fright – which, considering its treatment so far at the hands of humanity, he considered remarkable. On the other hand, it might have been that it simply had no choice. Tied to its tail by a piece of string was a large rock – no doubt to provide assistance on its journey to the floor of the pond.

'Poor thing!' Rosalind murmured, her eyes bright with unshed tears. 'How could anyone be so cruel to something so small and helpless?'

'I fear that smallness and helplessness are only spurs to violence and cruelty.'

'No one shall harm you now, little one.' She picked up the creature and stroked it gently, which seemed to be just the thing, for, wet as she was, the kitten rubbed its head against her hand and emitted that low rumble of sound peculiar to felines.

'It is an unusual beast,' St George commented, watching the two with a curious look on his face.

That it was. Not black nor white, not ginger, but a smoke-grey and eyes so pale a green they were almost yellow.

'What shall you do with' – he lifted a hind leg gingerly and inspected its posterior – 'her?'

'I shall take her home with me, of course.'

'And what will Welly think of that?'

Welly himself answered this question by waddling up to them at that very moment. He stuck his nose in the kitten's face, with more curiosity than malice. The kitten, in turn, reached out a velvety paw and placed it on said nose.

'Friendship at first sight.' St George eased himself up off of the ground and reached down to Rosalind.

'Thank God you are alive!' Cousin Priscilla reached their side slightly ahead of the others. 'I was never so frightened in all my life.'

'I do not think that I will ever set foot on a boat again.'

'Nonsense!' St George scoffed at this. 'You were quite enjoying yourself until you decided to go for a swim.'

Rosalind ignored his jest. Handing him the kitten, she reached out to Cassandra. 'My dear,' she cried, 'you are quite drenched.'

'So are you!'

'So are we all,' Julian said, 'except for the very sensible Mrs Plummer.'

'We had best get these young ladies home and into their beds before they catch a chill,' St George reminded them.

'Trust you to know what to do!' Cousin Priscilla beamed upon him with approval.

They made their way back to their makeshift pavilion and the blankets upon which they had been seated earlier were transformed into large wraps to protect the two wet damsels.

'But what about yourselves?' Cassandra asked, perturbed by the gentlemen's carelessness toward the elements.

'Do not worry about us, dearest,' Julian replied tenderly. 'As long as you are well, so will we be.'

It was a very different looking party which made its way back to the abbey. Their clothes were dampened but their spirits were as high as ever. Indeed, they were laughing at one of St George's witticisms as they pulled up before the great stone building. Before they could even open the door of the barouche, however, the door of the abbey swung open and a figure appeared out of the semi-gloom.

A silence fell over the group as they observed this person – a stranger to at least three of them: a broad-shouldered, rather stocky gentleman with a balding pate and an exceedingly grim countenance.

'What is it?' Cassandra asked, wondering aloud at the air of hushed expectancy around her.

'I should like to know,' the figure spoke, and its tone was not precisely welcoming. 'I should like very much to know what you have been up to, my dear Cassandra.'

Cassandra's mouth and eyes seemed to be vying to see which could open the widest. There was such a shocked look upon her face that the fact of her blindness was harder than ever to credit. But the cause of her stupefaction became clear when she uttered one single, breathless word:

'Papa!'

CHAPTER FIFTEEN

Whenever there is a heavy shower of rain, there are always those who will say that it is 'coming down in buckets'. That evening it came down in barrels. Looking out through the windows of the lodge, Julian could see nothing but occasional flickers of light reflected from the drops by the glow of the lamps in the drawing-room. It was past midnight on as gloomy and unpropitious a night as one could imagine, and the two men were alone together with no companion other than a bottle of brandy. Mrs Plummer had bid them goodnight more than an hour ago.

'Do come away from the window,' St George urged him. 'You have been standing there for a quarter of an hour at least, like a sentry expecting the enemy to attack at any moment. It is most annoying.'

'I am contemplating my future,' his friend said mournfully. 'And a bleak one it is too.'

'You have missed your calling.' Richard leaned his head against the tips of his fingers, as though in the throes of a violent headache. 'You should have been on the stage.'

Julian finally swung around, letting fall the heavy satin curtain which he had been holding aside to peer out into the darkness.

'I would not expect you to understand.' His tone was a mixture of irritation and stoic resignation. 'You have never been in love.'

'No,' Richard admitted, looking across at Julian as he threw himself down upon the opposing chair. 'That is one disease with which I have never been afflicted.'

'What am I to do!'

'Have a little more of this excellent brandy,' Richard advised practically.

Julian followed his advice, swallowing a mouthful much too quickly. If there was any benefit to be derived from this, it was not immediately apparent. He looked more hopelessly dejected than ever.

'I love her, Richard,' he said presently.

'I take it that you refer to Miss Woodford.'

'Naturally.'

'How could it be otherwise?'

'She is an angel. Such beauty, such grace, such intelligence! Her voice, her air, her manners – everything about her is absolute perfection.'

'A paragon, certainly,' St George agreed, though not without a suspicious twitch at the corners of his mouth. 'The only flaw which she possesses is one so insignificant that one scarcely likes to mention it: she is blind.'

'Do you think I care two straws about that!' Julian's indignation was as impassioned as his praises of the young lady. 'What man who knows Cassandra could fail to adore her?'

'At least one that I know of,' St George muttered under his breath, unnoticed by the younger man. Aloud he merely pointed out, 'I grant that she is lovely and amiable. But do you really think that your esteemed parents would rejoice at your alliance with a woman who is not merely blind, but – perhaps even more importantly – the daughter of a mere Yorkshire merchant?'

Julian frowned. 'I own it may not be the kind of match which they had hoped for—'

'That, I would say, is a masterful understatement.' St George swirled the brandy in his glass, contemplating it as if it were an oracle. 'There are several peers, including at least one indigent earl, who have been throwing their daughters at your feet these past few months. If you wished to marry, any one of these would be a much more advantageous alliance.'

'To hell with earls and their platter-faced daughters!' Julian cried, the brandy beginning to have its effect after all. 'I shall have Cassandra or no one.'

'There is one very large fly in your ointment, I would say.'

'Mr Woodford.' Julian subsided limply against the back of his seat, immediately following his friend's train of thought.

That Miss Woodford's father was not impressed with either of the two gentlemen had been painfully apparent that after-noon. He allowed neither of them more than a few hesitant words before ordering them to quit his property instantly. He told them that he required no introductions and, taking the arm of each of the two sodden young women, had marched them into the house and slammed the door firmly in the faces of the three visitors. While nobody could describe him as a gracious host, neither could anyone accuse him of being a hypocrite. He dismissed them with such unconcealed contempt that St George found himself warming to him at once.

'I do not think that Papa Woodford will look kindly upon your suit,' he remarked idly. 'Indeed, I suspect that you will not be permitted entry into the abbey under any circumstances. Mr Woodford stands as an angel with flaming sword, guarding the entrance to Eden.'

'I shall gain admittance,' Julian vowed, growing ever more melodramatic, 'if I have to scale the walls with my bare hands!'

'And, presuming you are granted an audience with the man,' Richard said, leaning forward a little to look him directly in the eyes, 'are you going to reveal the true reason for our presence here in the country, and how we came to meet his daughter in the first instance?'

Julian groaned. 'That damned wager! If only I could turn back the clock, I would never have accepted something so outrageous.'

'In which case,' St George pointed out, 'you would never have met Cassandra at all.'

'How can I redeem myself?' He was the picture of desperation. 'How can I make myself acceptable to Mr Woodford?'

'Are you even certain that Cassandra would accept an offer if you made one?' St George countered.

Julian hesitated for a moment. 'I think – that is, I am almost certain that she has some feelings for me.'

'Have you ever kissed her?'

'No.'

'I never took you for such a slow-top, my boy.'

'Have you kissed Rosalind?' Julian returned, stung.

'That is hardly relevant at the moment.'

Julian gave a grunt which might almost have been construed as laughter had he not looked so utterly dejected. 'A fine pair of seducers we are!'

'As far as our wager goes, I think we must admit defeat.' St George shrugged carelessly. 'For my part, it has ceased to be amusing.'

'Have you any heart at all?' Julian marvelled at his lack of concern.

'Hearts are dangerous accoutrements,' his friend replied.

'They are too apt to be broken, as you are like to discover.'

'At any rate, my uncle is welcome to his money. I am glad we lost this wager. Are not you?'

'My fortune is large enough that I can well afford the loss.'

'Is money all that matters to you?' Julian was obviously growing irritated by this cool demeanour.

'Do not play the moralist now, my lad.' St George stood up and stretched lazily, like a restless cat. 'It ill becomes you.'

'Perhaps I am learning too late that those moralists I have been apt to deride are closer to the truth than I.'

'In that case, there is only one thing to be done.'

'What is that?'

St George looked down upon him. 'Gird your loins, acquit yourself like a man, and make a push to prostrate yourself before Papa Woodford and his daughter. When all else fails, sometimes one must resort to telling the truth. After that, it is in God's hands.'

While the two men were engaged in this unusual conversation, the ladies at the abbey were conducting one remarkably similar in nature. Having been subjected to a stony silence by Mr Woodford, they had been banished to their bedchambers with instructions to have a hot bath and rest. The inquisition could wait until the morrow. This threat did nothing to quiet the nerves of either girl; so, when Cassandra stole away to Rosalind's chamber at midnight, opening the door just wide enough to speak through the aperture, she found the room's occupant wide awake.

'Lindy!' she whispered, so as not to arouse anyone else. 'Are you awake?'

'Yes.' Rosalind also kept her voice low. The room was in darkness, but that would make no difference to Cassandra.

'Come in, Cass, and close the door behind you.'

She followed Rosalind's instructions and made her way cautiously to the bed. Seated side by side, they were both silent for several minutes. Cassandra drew up her knees to her chest, and wrapped her arms around them. In her white linen night garments, she was easy to spy even in the dim light trickling through the window.

'Papa is very angry,' she said at last.

'With good reason,' Rosalind answered. She had been lying on her side when Cassandra entered, but had pushed herself up in bed and leaned her back against the headboard.

'Do you think that he will permit Julian and Richard to visit us?'

'No.'

'Pray do not try to spare my feelings, Lindy!' Cassandra said pettishly. 'Tell me honestly what you feel.'

'Your father could hardly have arrived at a less propitious moment.' Rosalind recalled the scene with something of the feeling that the survivor of a shipwreck might view the ocean. 'The two of us drenched from head to toe – and the gentlemen in no better condition themselves. One can only guess what he must have been thinking.'

'I shall never see Julian again!' Cassandra sniffed, and Rosalind knew that her cheeks must be wet with tears.

'You never *have* seen him.' She attempted to treat the matter lightly, but their old jests were no longer amusing.

'I love him, Lindy.'

'No!' Rosalind's vehement cry caused the other to turn towards her sharply. 'You cannot love such a man. You love only what you have imagined him to be. You have never been courted by a man before, and naturally it has turned your head. But only think what he really is – what we know him to be –

and you will soon forget this foolish fancy.'

A piercing, heart-wrenching cry was the only answer to this. It did not come from Cassandra, however, but from the kitten, who was feeling much neglected on the floor of the bedchamber. With some consternation, Rosalind looked down into the darkness. The kitten, catching hold of the bedclothes draped over the side, climbed up in a flash and deposited herself on Rosalind's lap.

'What have you named her?' Cassandra asked, with a ridiculous descent into the mundane.

'I thought Lady Hamilton. She seems to have an affinity with men and with water.'

'Appropriate, but quite a mouthful.' Cassandra considered the matter. 'Since Welly is named for the Duke, perhaps we should simply call her Duchess.'

She reached out one hand in the general direction of the purring sound on the bedclothes, and received the rough wetness of Duchess's tongue. The cat's intervention seemed to have soothed her. Her tears ceased and she answered more rationally.

'My feeling for Julian is not a fancy. Nor do I think either of them so bad as they have been portrayed to us. If they were, neither of us could be so drawn to them.'

'Us!' Rosalind was determined to dispel this myth. 'I have no feeling for either gentleman but irritation.'

Cassandra gave a genteel kind of snort, indicating patent disbelief. 'You may lie to yourself, Lindy,' she said, 'but you cannot pull the wool over *my* eyes.'

'My emotions may not be entirely untouched,' Rosalind confessed. 'However, I am certain that once they are removed from our vicinity, we shall both soon be thankful that they are gone.'

'Dearest.' Cassandra was quiet and resigned as she leaned her head on her friend's shoulder. 'Dearest, you know as well as I do that you are speaking nonsense. For good or for ill, neither of us will ever be quite the same. For my part, I will never regret having known them.'

But Julian had never kissed Cassandra, Rosalind thought. She had never looked deep into his eyes and felt as though she were falling into them – into him. Oh, why had Richard St George ever come into her life? What could ever come of it but misery?

'I wish I had never laid eyes on either one of them!' she cried honestly.

'If only Papa had not returned so soon,' Cassandra mused. 'At least we might have had a few more days with them.'

'Indeed.'

'I wonder what made him change his plans?'

'I did.'

'What!'

Cassandra drew away from her friend with such violence that it startled Duchess, who gave a loud 'mew' as if to scold her for such inconsiderate behaviour. The young girl sat up in bed, turning her face towards her friend as if she could read every line and curve of her countenance.

'I wrote to him the night we walked out into the garden,' Rosalind said, the words like lead on her tongue.

'But why?'

Much to her own consternation, Rosalind felt the tears begin to stream down her cheeks. She could not remember the last time she had wept. She had always despised women who cried at every little disappointment, and the lugubrious heroines in romance novels were the brunt of many jokes she had shared with Cassandra. To find herself behaving like one of them was disconcerting, to say the least.

149

'I had to do it, Cass!' She sniffed loudly. The kitten gave up and scampered off to the end of the bed for a more peaceful doze. 'I did not know how long I could – I could resist him, if I did not.'

Suddenly the two women were clinging together, each aware of the other's sorrow and each attempting to ease it by whatever pitiful and unsuccessful means they could employ. It was a very long time before they both fell asleep.

CHAPTER SIXTEEN

The sunlight streaming through the open window the next morning was not welcome. Rosalind hoisted heavy eyelids like useless sails on a ship becalmed in the Doldrums. She lay mute and motionless, staring up at the ceiling and trying to summon enough spirit to rise and face the day. Finally, by a supreme effort of will, she swung her legs to the starboard side of the bed and now sat staring at the wall – which was slightly more interesting, as it had an oval mirror which reflected her own image. She looked like a female Robinson Crusoe, cast up on the bed like human flotsam on the shores of some far-off Pacific isle.

'What time is it?'

Her exertions had disturbed Cassandra, who yawned and stretched lazily.

'It must be past nine o'clock in the morning,' Rosalind warned her.

'So late?'

'It was almost daylight when I fell asleep.'

'Poor Lindy!' Cassandra was instantly concerned. 'And now we must face Papa.'

That was an evil event which could not be put off much

longer. Both women did their best, however, taking many minutes to choose an outfit and giving their maids as much trouble as possible over the arrangement of their coiffures. They each sipped a tepid cup of coffee and nibbled halfheartedly at a couple of scones before discarding them. At last there was nothing more to be done. Either they must remain confined to their bedchambers or venture out to meet their fate.

Coming down the stairs arm-in-arm, it seemed that they might yet have a slight reprieve. The hall below was empty. Even as this thought occurred to Rosalind, a plump figure popped out of a doorway and trotted toward them. It was Ellen, who greeted them at the foot of the stairs with this portentous announcement:

'The master wants to see you in the drawing-room. You'd best not keep him waiting.'

'Both of us?' Cassandra asked hopefully.

'Yes, Miss Woodford. Both of you.'

Mr Woodford was discovered pacing back and forth about the room, his hands clasped behind his back. The dour look on his face gave Rosalind a moment's pause, but she drew a deep breath and calmly bid her uncle good morning. He returned her greeting somewhat gruffly. Cassandra, eager to pacify and – if at all possible – disarm him, went forward with her arms out. He embraced her briefly, but was plainly too perturbed to be easily distracted from his purpose.

'Perhaps,' he said eventually, 'it would be best if I spoke to Rosalind alone.'

'Sending me away will serve no purpose,' his daughter informed him. 'You will merely put me to the trouble of listening outside the door.'

This halted him for a moment, but was hardly designed to mollify him.

'I have been too lax with you – with both of you,' he began. 'Allowing you to read whatever you please, indulging you beyond what is proper.' Here he paused, planting his feet firmly and adopting the belligerent stance which inevitably preceded one of his famous lectures.

'I know not by what arts these fiends have insinuated themselves into your acquaintance. You cannot possibly be aware of the kind of black-hearted knaves you have allowed to enter this hallowed haven of peace and tranquillity. I thought you safe here behind these noble walls, little thinking how the wiles of the serpent can so easily beguile the innocent. I had at least expected some measure of good sense from Rosalind—'

'And you see,' Cassandra interrupted, 'that you were right to do so.'

'Eh?' He was quite thrown out of his stride by this.

'Was it not Lindy's letter which brought you home to rescue us from these – these rakehells?'

'You should not be using such language, Cassy.' His tone reverted to that of the exasperated parent, before he turned to address the older woman. 'You should never have allowed them to be admitted within these walls, Rosalind.'

'I assure you, Uncle—'

'I was the one who let them in,' Cassandra confessed. 'Nor do I regret it in the least. We have had the most fun! Have we not, Rosalind?'

'Daughter!' King Lear never looked so stupefied at the thanklessness of Cordelia. 'Can I believe what I am hearing? After I read the letter which the uncle of this young jackanapes so kindly committed to me, I found it hard enough to believe that either of you could have been so foolish—'

He would undoubtedly have prosed on at much greater length, but was stopped by a commotion from the end of the hall. Someone was at the front door remonstrating with Debenham. The voice was clearly that of Julian Marchmont, and it was not difficult to discern that he intended to do whatever was necessary to gain admittance.

'I must speak with Mr Woodford. I shall not leave until I have done so!'

An unintelligible response from Debenham was followed by the sound of shuffling footsteps approaching. Debenham appeared in the drawing-room doorway, and had the pleasure of an audience which, though small, hung upon his every word. Alas, his words were few.

'Mr Julian Marchmont desires—'

That was the full extent of his speech, for Julian had quietly followed behind him and could now be seen by those in the drawing-room. At the same moment, Debenham realized that he was not alone. This was what halted his announcement – which, in any case, was now superfluous. Mr Marchmont himself was about to declare his desires for himself.

'How dare you enter this house, sir!'

Mr Woodford's heroic stance would have gained applause at Covent Garden. He might have been the Commendatore's statue stepping forward to drag Don Giovanni down to the nether regions. But Julian seemed unwilling to act the Don. He did not raise his voice, but his determination was evident to all.

'Mr Woodford, sir,' he said. 'I beg you to hear me out before you evict me from your house.'

'I fail to see, sir, what you can have to say which would in any way alter my intentions.'

'I wish to explain—'

'Your explanations,' Mr Woodford said grandly, 'are quite unnecessary. Your uncle's letter laid bare your scheme with remarkable clarity.'

'My uncle's letter?' the younger man repeated, obviously mystified.

It was Rosalind who answered him this time.

'Before you arrived in Buckinghamshire,' she explained, 'I received a letter from Sir Jasper Marchmont. It was directed to my uncle, but I had been instructed to open any correspondence which might arrive for him in his absence.'

For the first time Julian was made aware of the duplicitous nature of his uncle's scheme. His astonishment and chagrin as Rosalind related the rest of her tale could not be doubted. It seemed as though the revelation had robbed him of the ability to speak, and he swallowed before he did so, as though clearing his throat of some obstruction.

'I cannot deny,' he ventured at last, 'that my intentions when I came here were the very reverse of what is open and honourable. There is no defending the arrogance and heartless-ness of such an enterprise.'

'I am glad to see,' Mr Woodford said, 'that you are capable of expressing such sentiments, though I am far from being convinced that they are genuine, since your behaviour, thus far, has been unlikely to produce any confidence in anything which you might either say or do.'

'At least grant that I may be capable of more tender feelings than my conduct would indicate.' Julian was looking down at the rich parquet flooring as he spoke, but he raised his head to continue. 'If I cannot excuse what I have done, at least allow that I may be able to repent of it.'

Mr Woodford inclined his head in gracious acknowledgement that this might indeed be possible. Rosalind could see that he was wavering before responding to Julian's words, and could almost read his mind at that moment. Should he offer a speech of gracious absolution for the young man's sins? Should he deliver an oration on the dangers of pride, disdaining the young man's plea for mercy and dismissing him from his sight forever? Which would have the most dramatic effect? It was a difficult decision. In the end, he must have decided that magnanimity was most suited to his situation – tempered by a short sermon on the dissipated habits of the younger generation, of course.

'Far be it from me to withhold that degree of charity which all good Christian men should display in the face of such a petition.' He paused to make a pontifical gesture. 'I suppose that you are no worse than most of the fashionable fribbles which pollute the streets of town and have so lowered the moral tone of our Great Empire, even now sowing the seeds of our own future destruction.

'At least you are man enough to stand and face those whom you have wronged, and to offer an apology – though perhaps too little and too late. Go on your way, and let me see no more of you.'

'That I cannot do, sir,' Julian answered.

'What?' This was clearly not the response which the older man had expected. This Marchmont fellow was definitely not playing the part as it should be done. This was the cue for his exit. Why did he linger?

'I have a favour to beg of you, Mr Woodford – one which I do not deserve, admittedly.'

'What do you mean?'

'I wish to marry your daughter, sir. May I have your permission to pay my addresses to her?'

'Yes! Yes, you may!'

This immediate and most gratifying response did not issue from the lips of Mr Woodford however, but from Cassandra.

'Silence, girl!' This was probably the harshest tone Mr Woodford had ever used to her in all her life. 'Have you taken leave of your senses, sirrah?' he demanded next, addressing her suitor.

'If it be madness to be deep in love,' Julian said, 'then yes, I have taken leave of my senses. For I am very much in love with your daughter.'

'Oh, Julian!'

That Cassandra was much affected by this declaration was obvious to Rosalind. Her eyes might be sightless, but none could mistake the joy shining from them like a beacon. Her lips trembled and two tears, like cut crystal, dangled on the edge of each pink-tinged cheek. She had never looked so beautiful. It occurred to Rosalind that, in these few weeks, Cassandra had left her girlhood behind her and emerged as a young woman who knew what it was to love and to be loved.

That Mr Woodford was also much affected was equally plain. Pleasure, however, was not his dominant emotion. He was extremely angry at such brazen boldness. Where Cassandra had turned a delicate shade of pink, his face was bedecked in an unattractive shade of purple. The veins in his neck stood out like ropes, and she feared an attack of apoplexy.

'By God, sir!' he cried, forgetting his usual eloquence, 'I've a good mind to thrash the life out of you! You dare to come here and ask me – ME – for my daughter's hand? Get out of my house now, sir, while you still have two sound legs to stand on.'

'I do not wish to offend one whom I hope will someday be my father-in-law,' Julian answered, standing his ground, 'but if your daughter loves me, sir, then nothing and nobody shall prevent me from making her my wife.'

'Julian, I do love you!' Cassandra cried impetuously. 'I love you with all my heart.'

At this, the fierce look left the young man's face, to be replaced by a tenderness which was unmistakable. Whatever his original intentions might have been in paying court to Cassandra, they were long forgotten. His love was real. Rosalind did not doubt it for an instant, incredible though it seemed.

'You are both mad!' Mr Woodford's native Yorkshire brogue, which he generally took such pains to suppress, became much more pronounced. 'Ye'd better mind yourself, me girl. I've no patience with such cantrips.'

Rosalind considered that it was time for her to intervene. What the result might be, she could not guess. But someone had to be rational if there was any chance for a happy resolution to this hobble in which they found themselves.

'Uncle,' she said calmly, 'I think that you should consider carefully before you deny Mr Marchmont's request.'

'Eh?' Mr Woodford looked both confused and dismayed at what he clearly perceived as an act of betrayal on the part of his niece.

'Only consider, sir,' she expanded upon her theme, 'what an advantageous match this must be for Cassandra. Mr Marchmont comes from a family of impeccable lineage – in far more exalted circles than our own. Nor do you need to fear that he is after your daughter's fortune, since his own is at least as great.'

A reluctant 'harrumph' was all the response she got from her auditor.

'I believe that he is sincere in his devotion to Cassandra,

despite the inauspicious beginning to their acquaintance.' She clenched her hands together, moving a step nearer to her uncle and ignoring the other two in the room. 'She clearly loves him equally well. And should not her happiness be your greatest concern?'

There was a moment of silence. The two lovers waited breathlessly for his reaction to this.

'But she is just a child!' The father in him was very much in evidence, reluctant to part with his cherished image of a school-room miss at his knees.

'I think not, sir,' Rosalind told him, gently but firmly.

'And have you forgotten her condition?' He turned back to Julian. 'Are you willing to bear the burden of having to care for her for the rest of her life? Can you accept what your friends and family will say?'

'Sir,' Julian Marchmont answered him without hesitation, 'I can imagine no greater felicity than to care for and to cherish your daughter as long as we both shall live. My family will undoubtedly adore her, and anyone who would pity me, or slight her, is no friend of mine.'

'It is hard for me to believe that such a man as you can make her happy,' Mr Woodford protested. If his words lacked diplomacy, they compensated for it with refreshing honesty.

'If I do not marry Julian,' Cassandra told him, 'I shall never be happy again. You have given me so much, Papa. Do not deny me the one thing that I want – nay, that I *need* – most.'

Julian was about to add his plea to Cassandra's but stopped abruptly at a telling look from Rosalind. Reining in his passion, he proceeded more sedately.

'I beseech you most humbly, sir,' he requested, 'not to take from me the hope that you will at least consider my offer, which I make with all my heart.'

With the three of them ranged against him, what could the poor man do?

'Very well,' he said. 'I will think on it tonight, and let you know my decision tomorrow.'

They wisely refrained from any display of happiness at this victory. It would not do to antagonize the older man. Instead, Julian bowed and withdrew with no more than a loving glance at Cassandra and a smile of gratitude for Rosalind. Those two soon dismissed themselves as well, staying out of Mr Woodford's way for the rest of the day.

'Oh, thank you, Lindy. Thank you!' Cassandra embraced her friend as soon as they were alone together. 'I did not expect you to become our champion.'

'I do believe that he loves you,' Rosalind admitted, 'and I was not afraid to say so.'

'But will it serve, do you think? Will Papa really give us his blessing?'

'My uncle is no fool,' Rosalind reminded her, 'else he could not have become so wealthy in his business dealings. I think, once he considers the benefits of the match, he will come around.'

'And we shall owe it all to you!'

'Nonsense.'

'I am so happy.' Cassandra flung herself upon her bed and bounced up and down like a child. 'I never dreamed that I should ever be married. Can it possibly be true?'

'Miracles do happen, my dear – even today.'

'But what of you?' she asked, suddenly sober.

'Do not worry about me.' If her smile went somewhat awry, at least Cassandra could not see it. 'I shall be an old maid, sitting quietly with my cat, and a fond aunt to your children.'

'No.' Cassandra shook her head decisively. 'I am sure that you can do better than that.'

'Perhaps,' Rosalind conceded, trying for a lighter note. 'After all, there may yet be a Mr Plummer in my future.'

CHAPTER SEVENTEEN

In one thing, at least, Rosalind proved to be a reliable judge. On the following day Cassandra's father summoned Julian to the abbey. He arrived with Mrs Plummer and Richard St George, to whom Mr Woodford was at last properly introduced. He received them with great cordiality, which Rosalind recognized at once as a most auspicious sign. She was almost positive now that he had perceived the good sense of her arguments and was prepared to accept the young man as a prospective son-in-law.

As confirmation of her suspicions, Mr Woodford soon requested that Mr Marchmont accompany him to his study for a few moments. This left the other four occupants of the room to pass the time in commonplace comments upon the weather, although all of them were almost certainly preoccupied with their own speculations as to the outcome of the discussion taking place within the study walls.

Cassandra was nervous and distracted, several times having to be called to task by Rosalind for ignoring some question or remark by the others. For her part, Rosalind directed her gaze steadily towards Mrs Plummer, trying unsuccessfully to forget the presence of her nemesis a few feet away.

'It is a lovely day, is it not?' Rosalind enquired of the lady.

'Quite divine!' Mrs Plummer was eager as ever to comment upon anything and everything. 'A perfect day for a picnic – though not, perhaps, by the pond.'

'That might be tempting fate, indeed,' St George replied. He looked rather sour and his tone was more caustic than usual.

'I have spent such an enjoyable visit,' his cousin rhapsodized. 'I am quite distressed to think of it ending.'

'You are not leaving so soon?' Rosalind asked, genuinely surprised.

'Well,' the older woman shrugged regretfully, 'St George will be returning to Town tomorrow, and I am, after all, entirely at his disposal.'

'We will miss you greatly,' Rosalind said, and meant it.

'And how I shall miss my new friends here in Bucking-hamshire.' Mrs Plummer reached across to take her hand. 'Dear Miss Powell, you cannot guess how little your friend-ship has meant to me – and Miss Woodford too, of course! I trust that this will not be the first time we see each other again.'

'The day is indeed fine,' St George said, attempting to stem the flooding tide. 'A stroll in the garden would not go amiss.'

'An excellent idea!' Cousin Priscilla rose at once. 'Alas that it should be our last together. Such larks as we have had—'

Here she broke off her effusions, for the other two gentlemen had returned. The glow of Julian's countenance told Rosalind everything she needed to know. Her uncle beamed upon them also, in self-satisfied serenity.

'Cassandra, my dear,' he announced, 'I believe that Mr Marchmont wishes to have a word with you in private.'

'Of course!' She almost flew up from her seat. 'Shall we use your study, sir?'

'Surely there is no need,' St George said smoothly. 'We were just planning to enjoy the gardens, which are quite enticing on such a day. Stay where you are, and we shall remove ourselves forthwith.'

To the surprise of the quartet which ventured out of doors, the sun was no longer shining. A light breeze had sprung up which, if it did not exactly shake 'the darling buds of May', at least ruffled the delicate blooms of August. Low grey clouds spread out across the sky like spilt water on a polished blue table.

Whether by contrivance or by chance, Rosalind found herself partnered by St George while her uncle was fully engaged with Mrs Plummer. In a very few minutes, St George's faster pace had separated them a considerable distance from the dilatory tread of the older couple. In fact, they arrived at the cloisters where their very first meeting had taken place. Rosalind wondered whether she would ever behold this particular place without remembering that momentous occasion.

Thus far they had not spoken. This was unusual enough, for they never met but what they bandied words about like tennis balls. His silence was strangely ominous, threatening a thunderbolt. Never had she seen his brow so darkly furrowed, his eyes so hard and cold. Still he did not speak, and the silence unnerved her so that she felt she must say something – anything! – or go mad.

'So, you are leaving the country then,' she remarked.

'My reason for being here is now at an end.'

'And what reason was that?'

'Your seduction, of course.' He did not flinch, did not offer an apology. The words were uttered with complete unconcern.

'You retire in defeat?' How she got the words out without choking, she did not know.

'I was unaware that you were well informed of our intentions

164

even before we arrived.'

'Julian has told you of his uncle's letter.' It was a statement, not a query.

He did not deny it. 'It seems,' he said, with some degree of self-mockery, 'that while we thought ourselves to be playing a deep game, you and Miss Woodford were playing an even deeper one.'

'Sir Jasper acted somewhat the part of a guardian angel, in fact.'

'I would not impute to him so altruistic a motive.' His chuckle was not one of amusement, but rather of incredulity.

'What do you mean, sir?'

In their perambulation, they had now arrived at the small arbour with the armillary where Rosalind had come so perilously near the precipice of her own wayward desires. He drew away from her and stepped around so that once again they faced each other across it. There was no beguiling moonlight now, but only the harsh rays of the sun, interrupted now and then by the passing of clouds overhead and the distant rumble of thunder.

'From what I have heard,' St George told her, 'it would appear that Julian's uncle acquainted you with all the details of our little wager – with one notable exception.'

'And what was that?'

'He neglected to tell you that it was he himself who proposed the wager and told us about the forbidding abbey and its beautiful but mysterious inhabitants.'

'What!'

Rosalind could not deny that she was both shocked and appalled at this revelation. The man who had represented himself as the defender of their virtue and the upholder of pious morality was himself the one who had helped to bring this calamity upon them. It was incredible! Yet she did not doubt that what St George had told her was the truth. After all, now that she considered the matter, it was certainly odd that they should be using the man's home for their schemes. Knowing of it, he could easily have forbidden them to stay there. Why had that never occurred to her before? Not that it would have made any difference, she supposed. Their behaviour would have been the same in any event.

'So you see, you were not quite so clever after all, my dear dragon – were you?'

'I never pretended to be clever.' She lifted her chin and looked straight at him. 'Whatever I said or did was only what I thought best to protect myself and Cassandra from two men who were known to be rakes. That much I would have done even had I never received the letter.'

'Nevertheless, it seems that you had an unfair advantage over us.'

'Instead of the unfair advantage which you and Julian should have had over *us*?'

'Exactly so.'

'At least, since Sir Jasper was not entirely honest with you, I would imagine that the wager is now forfeit. Though you may have lost, you are not obliged to pay.'

'True.' His lip curled slightly. 'Trust a woman to think of such a thing. It had not even crossed my mind.'

'I suppose that you are too wealthy yourself for it to matter.'

'Indeed.'

There was silence again for several moments. The wind picked up, blowing the ribbons of her bonnet across her throat. She pushed them back, but to no avail. They returned again immediately.

'At least Cassandra has not been hurt,' she said at last. 'And

Julian seems content with the outcome of his adventure.'

'I wish them both very happy.' But he did not sound like it.

'*His* feelings, at least, were not entirely feigned.' Try as she might, she could not keep the hint of bitterness out of her voice.

'No,' he confessed. 'Though none of us, I think, can surpass your own performance.'

'I beg your pardon?'

'That night, here in the garden,' he reminded her. 'You were quite superb, you know. Even with my own vast experience of women, I was convinced that you cared for me. Believe me, Miss Powell, you are quite wasted here. You should be on the stage.'

'Thank you.' Her heart felt as though it had just been trampled under his feet, but she would die rather than let him see it. 'I did not suspect the extent of my own talents until you came here.'

'It has been a most – enlightening – experience.'

'I hope that you have learnt something by it.'

'Only that no man can match a woman when it comes to deceit.'

'Of that I am not so certain.'

Inevitably, their tête-à-tête was interrupted – and, as it happened, by the same voice which had ended their previous encounter.

'There you are!' Mrs Plummer cried. 'Mr Woodford is so knowledgeable about agriculture. He was telling me all about cultivating roses. Alas, it is all one to me! But certainly the gardens here are most delightful. I could leave here forever, and never wonder of seeing its tires.'

While the others tried to decipher this last sentence, they all began to move towards the house. They soon made their way back to the drawing-room, where they discovered the couple –

who could now be described as officially engaged – seated side by side on the sofa.

'Are congratulations in order?' St George asked his friend, with a raised brow.

'I am the happiest man alive!' Julian assured him.

What followed was the usual round of questions and felicitations. The ladies congregated on one side of the room and the men gathered on the other.

At last the most interesting subject was exhausted and the party from the lodge took their leave. Standing in the doorway with her uncle and Cassandra, Rosalind watched the barouche drive away. Tomorrow Richard St George would return to London. But certainly this was the last she would ever see of him. He swept out of her life as swiftly as he had swept into it. But how long, she wondered, would it be before she could banish him from her heart?

CHAPTER EIGHTEEN

As it happened, Julian requested that Mrs Plummer remain with him at the lodge until the wedding. She would be of great help to both himself and Cassandra during this brief period of their betrothal. Since the family at the abbey did not attend church – one of the things which had helped to fuel the fires of gossip in the village – it was decided not to have the banns published in the usual manner. Instead, Julian would travel to London to obtain a Special Licence.

The Woodfords had once employed a retired clergyman as their unofficial chaplain, who conducted services in the small lady chapel which was all that remained of the original abbey church. The old man had gone on to his reward some three years previously, and the services had ceased, although Mr Woodford read prayers in the chapel each Sunday when he was at home and the girls would generally choose one or two hymns to sing in honour of the Lord's Day.

The strong influence of the Evangelicals did not lead the family to look very kindly upon the Established Church. It was therefore a Herculean task to find anyone to conduct the wedding service for them. After conducting some enquiries round about the neighbouring county, Julian eventually discovered a Methodist minister in a nearby town. The Reverend

Austen Jenkins listened sympathetically as the young man explained the peculiar circumstances of his bride and her family, and expressed himself as being very pleased to consecrate their vows on a date to be determined by the parties concerned.

'Did you explain to Reverend Jenkins how you came to meet your betrothed?' Rosalind asked him, when he arrived at the abbey with his good news.

'I did not,' he answered simply. 'I am not a complete nodcock, you know. I wanted the man to marry us, not send me to the Devil!'

One of the strangest incidents over the course of the next fortnight was the return of Julian's uncle. Having now been fully informed as to the extent of his involvement in the whole sordid business which had brought Julian and St George into their small circle, it was with mixed emotions that Rosalind, Cassandra and Mr Woodford anticipated his introduction. It could not now be avoided, but it could yet be dreaded.

Julian arranged all by persuading his uncle to invite the party from the abbey to dine with them at the lodge one evening. That it would be awkward was beyond question; that it was inevitable was equally certain. The man was to be connected to them whether they approved of him or not, and, as Rosalind pointed out with her usual common sense, if they could forgive the nephew for his part, they could hardly refuse to pardon the uncle for instigating the affair. After all, his was only the suggestion; the performance depended upon others, who might easily have refused if their pride had not eclipsed their morals.

To everyone's surprise, they found Sir Jasper's charm to be quite irresistible. It was clear that Julian had inherited the most disarming qualities of his relation; Rosalind could only hope that the younger Marchmont was more respectable. She could not help but be entertained by Sir Jasper's wit and engaging manners, but suspected that his morals were rather less firm.

After dinner, she enjoyed an unexpected few minutes of private conversation with him, while Julian and Cassandra flirted and whispered on a sofa and Mrs Plummer distracted her uncle with more outrageous tales of her late unlamented husband.

'It seems, Miss Powell,' Sir Jasper commented, eyeing the young couple with a kind of detached approval, 'that all's well that ends well.'

'Even if it is not precisely the outcome which you antici-pated,' she remarked with gentle sarcasm.

'On the contrary.' He turned his gaze back towards her with a twinkle in his eye. 'This is very much what I expected, with one notable exception.'

'And what is that?' She could not help but be curious.

'That you are not yet engaged to my old friend, Richard St George.'

She stiffened immediately. 'I cannot conceive what you can mean by such a remark, sir.'

'Come, come, my dear child.' His look was far too knowing for her taste. 'It seems to me that you are just the sort of woman who could bring that hound to heel. I have been awaiting the announcement these three weeks or more.'

'Then you wait in vain, sir.'

'Would you care to wager on that?'

'You are far too apt to wager, Sir Jasper – particularly on the lives of others. Are we merely pawns in some game?'

If she meant to discomfit him, she did not succeed. He smiled slyly and, if anything, seemed to take her remark as some kind of compliment.

'I must admit,' he said, 'that my fellow creatures provide me with endless amusement.'

'And if someone should be hurt in the course of your schemes?'

'There is that, of course.' He shrugged carelessly. 'But we must all take our chances in the game of life. Some win, some lose, and some make fools of themselves to no purpose. I am a mere spectator, and I think that observing you and St George will provide me a pleasant diversion for some time to come.'

'Forgive me if I do not find it quite so droll as you do.'

'You are angry.' He shook his head in mock sadness. 'But remember that the game is not over yet. As in a horse race, my dear, many come from behind to pass the finish line in first place.'

Rosalind did not feel like a winning entry. She felt sad and lonely and hopelessly confused. How could she harbour tender feelings towards someone like Richard St George? It was madness. Yet something had gone out of her life along with him. He had stolen her peace of mind, tricked her into compromising her deepest convictions, and now fled with a rather large portion of her heart. Why was it that something inside of her still cherished the absurd belief that he was not what he seemed – that there was yet a heart beneath that carefully contrived exterior of cold calculation? Even after his vindictive appraisal of her that last day at the abbey, there was something – not precisely hope, but not entirely divorced from it – which taunted her with foolish fancies which were all but impossible to be true.

Cassandra could not help but notice her long-time companion's want of spirits. Nor did it require the genius of Isaac Newton to discern its cause. She could not stay silent on the subject, but confronted Rosalind with it at the earliest opportunity.

'If only,' she said wistfully, 'we could find someone for you, Lindy: a man who would value you as you truly deserve.'

'But where to hunt for such a mythical beast?' Rosalind attempted to disarm her with humour.

'I cannot be put off with witticisms,' Cassandra said, refusing to be placated. 'It pains me to know how you suffer for someone unworthy of your affection. Do you not remember how you always praised Elinor Dashwood as the only sensible heroine in any novel, when she declared that it was not possible for one's happiness to depend entirely on any particular person?'

'Did I do so?'

Cassandra sighed heavily. 'How often,' she mused aloud, 'we have talked late into the night of the books we were reading. The words of great writers have been our companions more than any flesh and blood humans.'

'We have been cut off from society almost all our lives,' Rosalind acknowledged. 'I am still undecided as to whether that were a good thing or not.'

'If Christ commands us to carry His gospel into all the world,' Cassandra argued, 'how can we do so if we lock ourselves away from it? How can we shut it out and still reach it?'

'You are right, Cass. For all your youth, you are wiser than I. My tongue may be clever, but my heart is as foolish as the most idiotish of heroines in all those absurd romance novels we have read.'

'So you are no longer inclined to agree with Elinor Dashwood?' Cassandra asked, sliding along the edge of the sofa and placing a sympathetic arm around Rosalind's shoulder.

'In theory,' Rosalind answered, 'I must still agree with her. My head tells me that she is right. But, as Shakespeare so rightly said, "There was never yet philosopher that could endure the toothache patiently".'

'Our hearts so often sabotage our heads,' Cassandra agreed. 'I do not wish to see your heart broken.'

'You shall not.' There was, perhaps, a degree of grim determination about this brave statement. 'My heart is bruised, certainly, but not so gravely that it will not recover. In time, I shall be myself again. I still have much to be thankful for, after all.'

'But it is so hard to be thankful when one is so dreadfully blue-devilled.'

'Whatever their colour, my devils will be banished at last.'

'I had rather they were banished at first.'

So their discussion ended. Neither was quite satisfied with the outcome. On the one hand, Cassandra doubted her friend's resilience. Despite her protestations, she felt that Rosalind would not recover so easily from this affair. Rosalind was more determined than ever to show no signs of her hurt and disappointment. She could not allow her own mortification to dim the brightness of Cassandra's happiness. Cassandra deserved to enjoy these halcyon days as much as any young bride. Who, in fact, deserved it more?

No, Rosalind resolved, she would not be a blight on the joyous preparations, but enter into them with an enthusiasm which she hoped she would be able to feign better than she had done so far. Had not St George himself commented upon her acting abilities? But then, he had been quite wrong. That night in the garden had probably been the one time in their acquaintance when all pretence had dissolved in the heat of a passion of which she had never dreamed. Now it was over and she must accept the role which had been handed to her.

'I shall not repine,' she whispered to herself. If she repeated that often enough, she might even begin to believe it.

CHAPTER NINETEEN

While Rosalind was nursing her wounds in the country, the man who had inflicted them was adopting another course of action entirely. She might be totally unaware of it, but Richard St George was not the heart-whole rake he had professed to be when he accepted Sir Jasper's wager. While she languished in Buckinghamshire, he was enjoying a season of unrivalled profligacy in London. He found out every cockfight and prize-fight, winning or losing enormous amounts without the least interest in either. He attended masked balls and lavish house parties thrown by the most exalted members of the *ton*. He was seen at the opera with a ladybird of dazzling plumage, and even graced the hallowed halls of Almack's with his presence – though the patronesses fixed eagle eyes upon him the entire time, lest he overstep by one inch the strict social boundaries observed there.

On one particular evening he visited Honoria Inchwood's establishment for the first time since the night when Sir Lester Malmsbury had demolished the ceiling. The damage had been repaired, and all was much as it had ever been.

Honoria herself greeted him with genuine affection. He had pulled her out of the River Tick on at least one occasion, and was one of the few gentlemen she regarded as more than a client: as a friend. She had heard tales of his exploits these past three weeks or more, but had dismissed most of them. Seeing him now, though, she confronted him with the latest *on-dits* which were titillating the town.

'Everyone's talking about you, Richard,' she said, looking him over with a critical eye. 'And it looks like they ain't fibsters either.'

'Let them talk.' He shrugged carelessly. 'Much do I care for them, either their praise or their censure.'

'There's talk of orgies and all sorts of goings-on.'

This coming from the abbess of a Covent Garden nunnery provoked a smile from him in spite of himself.

'Preaching morality, Honoria? Have you become an Evangelical?'

She ignored this slur. 'I only want to know what's the matter with you, that's all.'

'Nothing at all is the matter with me.' He downed a glass of wine in one gulp and collapsed on a chair in a dark corner of the room, eyeing with dull contempt the other occupants engaged in their usual debauchery.

'You're drinking too much.'

'I always drink too much.'

'Not you, Richard,' she contradicted with the casual assurance of an old friend. 'Oh, I've seen you drink your share, all right,' she conceded, 'but you never entered or left this house looking like a seasick sailor.'

'Things change, my dear.' His mouth twisted into something which might have been mistaken for a smile, but was not. 'I am indulging in a giddy round of unending pleasure.'

'You don't look to me like a man who's enjoying himself. And I ought to know, if anyone does!'

'And just what *do* I look like, Miss Inchwood?'

177

She looked him up and down for a moment, her eyes narrowed. It was a penetrating stare, and behind it there was a world of experience with the foibles of the opposite sex.

'I'd say,' she pronounced at last, 'that you have the look of a man who's been crossed in love. In fact, if it was anyone else, there'd be no doubt in my mind that a woman is behind all this wild carousing of yours.'

'I've also done my share of carousing before, I believe.'

'This is different,' she said confidently.

'Do you really think that a woman could ever have such power over me?'

She nodded sagely. 'It would have to be a very special woman. I'll grant you that.'

'And supposing,' he asked, his own eyes narrowed now, 'that such a unique creature existed. What would you suggest that I do about it?'

'Well, if you're as mad for her as you seem to be,' Honoria said bluntly, 'you'd best marry her – if she'll have you. Not but what she'd be a fool if she didn't!'

'Thank you, my dear Honoria. You make me feel not quite so worthless as I had assumed myself to be.'

He might not admit as much, but there was no doubt that Honoria was right. Later that evening, lying fully clothed upon his bed, having flung a boot at his valet's head for daring to enter his bedchamber, he faced the demon – or, more accurately, the dragon – which had been pursuing him these many weeks.

He reflected that he had been serving in India at the time of Waterloo; now he wished that he could have been there, so that he might have been blown to bits by Boney's damned artillery. Anything would be better than this unbearable torture. And all because of a silly chit of a girl! No, that was not quite true. She was not silly, and, though she looked younger than her years, she could not precisely be described as a girl. Rosalind Powell was a woman – a woman of strength and beauty and wit – and lips of which even now, if he closed his eyes, he could taste the sweetness. Damnation! She had no right to make him feel this way.

He should have known that night in the garden that he had gone too far. His tactics seemed to be working all too well as he drew her into his arms and pressed his mouth to hers. Though she hesitated at first, her response had startled him with its passion and promise. He had felt his desire rising, carrying them both along. He wanted her so desperately that he completely forgot the wager and everything else. There in the moonlight, it was he who was losing control, acting like a lovesick schoolboy. He had never allowed his emotions to over-rule his judgement – not since his salad days, at least. Perhaps not even then. But Rosalind made him feel things he had never felt before.

That day on the pond had been his moment of truth. When she fell into the pond and he saw her floundering and sinking, it needed no cry from Cassandra to propel him into the water. The thought of her lying cold and lifeless was like a living death. From that day onward, there was no denying the truth – at least to himself. He loved Rosalind Powell with every sinew of his soul. It was a development so unexpected, so unprecedented, that he was caught quite off guard. How had this happened?

From the beginning he had found her captivating. But he pushed his feelings aside with an inward smirk of self-derision. It was lust, that was all. He was accustomed to lust; he under-stood it. Lust was comfortable and familiar to him. But what he felt now was new and unfamiliar, and anything but comfort-

able. It was agony! To be desperate for the sound of one particular voice, the sparkle in a particular pair of eyes . . . it was
maddening. To desire someone else's happiness above your
own, to feel ashamed of everything in your past and unworthy
of even a touch from the one whose touch you wanted more
than life itself. What kind of lunacy was this?

At least on that day he had been assured that she felt desire
for him, even if she could not esteem him. It was not enough,
of course. He hungered for her good opinion, thirsted for her
to trust and admire him when she had every reason not to do
so. Then, when Julian returned and explained to him that the
two women had known of their plans all along, he was stunned.

He was angry to think that all along it was *they* who were
being duped by two clever young misses. And he was hurt – as
mortally wounded as if one of Miss Powell's arrows were
embedded in his very heart. For now he could only assume that
the passion Rosalind had displayed had been all an act. She
cared nothing for him. She despised him. That he deserved her
ill opinion was beside the point. It was unendurable to think
that she held him in contempt.

When he confronted her in the garden that last day at the
abbey, he was all bravado, determined to show her that it had
been nothing more than a diversion to him as well. He wrapped
himself in unconcern as in a cloak. Her cool reception of his
words confirmed his suspicions. She was glad to see him go, no
doubt. He had lost his wager and his heart, but never would he
let her guess her ultimate victory over him.

He fled back to London, prepared to fool everybody just as
he had Rosalind. Apparently, though, he was fooling only
himself. Honoria had sniffed out his heartache like a trained
hound after a scurrying fox. Did anyone else guess his secret
shame?

Two days later, he was at his club, morose and not inclined for company, when a familiar voice hailed him cheerfully.

'Well met, my boy!' Sir Jasper Marchmont dropped into the chair facing his own. 'Had enough of rustication, I take it?'

'It is all a waste of time,' Richard answered bleakly.

'Come now! You must admit that you enjoyed the thrill of the chase while it lasted.'

'To no purpose, however,' was the response. 'The quarry managed to escape, thanks to your own efforts.'

'You cannot blame a man for trying to tip the odds in his favour,' Sir Jasper reasoned, not in the least contrite.

'Some men would have called you out for less.'

'Fortunately, you are too wise – and too respectful of your elders.'

'Well, I suppose we got what we deserved.' St George tipped half a glass of brandy down his throat, not batting an eyelid.

'Julian is getting a wife out of the adventure,' Sir Jasper commented. 'How did you benefit?'

'Believe me, sir,' St George said, 'I have learnt a lesson which I shall not soon forget.'

'Your dear mama will be most disappointed to learn of the outcome,' the older man mused aloud.

'My mother?' Richard's brows drew together above his nose and his gaze sharpened. 'What has she to say to anything?'

Sir Jasper spread his hands in a gesture indicating a reluctant confession. 'Well,' he said, 'I could not resist letting your mother know about our little wager. About a week after you left for Buckinghamshire, I believe it was.'

'Really?' St George's lip curled ever so slightly. 'And how did she take it?'

'She was quite diverted.' Sir Jasper chuckled at the memory. 'She was even ready to wager that you would undoubtedly seduce Miss Powell, though she would not swear for Julian's success. She is monstrous proud of your accomplishments, you know.'

'My accomplishments!' His laugh was about as pleasant as curdled milk. 'They are great indeed.'

'You were wont to boast of them yourself,' Sir Jasper reminded him. 'That was the whole point of our wager, was it not?'

'A fool's wager, made by a pair of jackasses!'

Sir Jasper stood up, looking down at his friend with a twinkle in his eyes:

'He is no fool,' he remarked, 'who knows more about himself today than he did yesterday.'

CHAPTER TWENTY

In Buckinghamshire, things were well in train for the approaching nuptials. A modiste from London was brought down especially to make a new gown for Cassandra. Cousin Priscilla was as helpful as she knew how to be. Rosalind was her old, phlegmatic self – at least in public.

Julian had much to talk about with his intended and much to do. He was already making arrangements for the purchase of a house only two miles from the abbey, for he did not want to remove his bride too far from her father and Rosalind. He knew that, despite their love, there was bound to be a period of adjustment. It would be best for her if those nearest and dearest to her were close by when she needed them. Mr Woodford was much impressed by the young man's consideration, and delivered a particularly long-winded panegyric in his presence which Julian bore with great fortitude.

He had already ridden into Hampshire to inform his parents of his choice of bride. He even had the forethought to take a miniature of Cassandra for them to have some notion of her undeniable beauty. The Marchmonts took the news in their stride. A fairly large, liberal family, they were ready to embrace almost any girl their son might choose. Cassandra need not have worried on that head. That she was blind was hardly an impediment; that she was an heiress was a point decidedly in her favour. All in all, they could not have been happier, and looked forward to attending the wedding and staying at the abbey with as much delight as anyone could have reasonably wished for.

For these impetuous young lovers, the sweet sorrow of parting came yet again when Julian was forced to go up to London for the Special Licence – that article so necessary before the ceremony could take place. Besides, he must needs select a more suitable London house for those occasions when, as he fully intended, he should introduce his wife into broader society. Unlike Cassandra's father, there was no doubt in Julian's mind that her courage and good humour would be more than equal to such a task – especially with her husband at her side.

He was almost a week in the metropolis before he was able to accomplish one of his most important errands. He wanted to seek out St George and ask him to support him at the altar. It would scarcely seem complete if he were not there.

He found his old friend in his lodgings in Berkeley Square. Upon being admitted by the manservant, Julian entered eagerly, only to be brought up short at the sight which met his gaze. Never had he seen Richard St George in such an unkempt state. A disciple of Brummell, St George was always immaculately groomed. It was apparent at once that he needed a shave, and possibly a bath as well. His hair looked as though he had done no more than run his fingers through it. He slouched in an uncomfortable-looking chair, with an empty bottle of wine on the table beside him, and ordered his man to bring another for him and his guest.

'Thank you, no,' Julian said, taking a seat opposite him.

'A staid married man already, I see,' St George sneered.

'I cannot stay long.'

'Must run back to Miss Woodford's skirts, eh?'

Julian was still in shock as he continued to take in his friend's dishevelled condition.

'What ails you, man?' he demanded at last, coming abruptly to the point. 'You look like the devil.'

'Thank you, kind friend.' Richard executed a sloppy bow in acknowledgement of this.

'I tried to find you at your club, but was informed that you had not been there for several days.'

'I have not been out of this house for – how long is it now, Brenton?'

'Three days, sir.' The manservant, his face wooden, answered the carelessly thrown question.

'I think you should see a physician, Richard.'

'You think I'm like to stick my spoon in the wall?' He laughed and choked all at once. 'I'm not that far gone yet.'

'You look much as I imagine the late Mr Plummer must have looked when in his cups,' Julian said frankly.

'How is my dear Cousin Priscilla?' His lip curled in a way that jarred Julian's nerves. 'All a-twitter with all the wedding plans, I would imagine.'

'That is what I came to see you about.'

'Cousin Priscilla?' St George asked. 'Send her packing back to Kent, if you like. What do I care?'

'I came to ask if you would support me at the wedding,' Julian responded between clenched teeth. Really, he wondered whether he should even ask him. If this was how he was going on, his presence would hardly be an asset.

'Thank you for the offer.' Still that harsh, mocking tone, Julian noted. 'I am in no mood for such festivities, however.'

Suddenly, a great light dawned upon the younger man. Perhaps because he himself was so newly introduced to the pains and pleasures of love, he realized that the problem with the man before him was of the heart rather than with any other organ of the body. St George had made few comments about Miss Powell in those last weeks in the country. In fact, Julian knew not how far he had progressed in his attempt to seduce her. Could it be that the slipper was on the other foot? They had both set out as hunters. Was it possible that, just as he had been captured by his own quarry, Richard had similary succumbed to the not inconsiderable charms of Miss Powell? Let him attempt a small test . . . .

'It seems that we shall be a very small party indeed, since Miss Powell also is likely to be absent.'

'I cannot see her missing Cassandra's wedding,' the other man commented, clearly surprised.

'I'm afraid Miss Powell is most unwell.'

'Unwell!' St George straightened at once, the dull look dispelled from his eyes. 'How so? She was fine when I left Buckinghamshire.'

'She has a generally strong constitution, to be sure. But perhaps her tumble into the pond, and the stress of losing Cassandra's constant companionship . . . the physician speaks of consumption . . . .'

'Consumption' The wine and the chair were both forgotten. Suddenly the older man was pacing about the room. 'Good God!' he cried. 'Why did no one inform me of this before? If anything should happen to Rosalind—'

'Quiet yourself, sir.' Julian stood up and faced his friend. 'Miss Powell may be a trifle fatigued with all the preparations, but otherwise I assure you she is perfectly well.'

St George stared at his friend in astonishment. 'What in

God's name do you mean by this, Julian? By God, if you are lying to me, I swear—'

'What I told you first about Rosalind was a lie,' Julian admitted. 'But your reaction has confirmed what I suspected. You are in love with her, Richard!'

'Go to the devil!'

Julian snorted. 'I see you do not deny it.'

'Go back to your bride,' St George answered wearily, collapsing once more on to the chair.

'You *do* love her,' Julian repeated, ignoring his friend's rude request. 'For the Lord's sake, man, why did you not tell her so? If I could have the temerity to offer for Cassandra, surely you could have plucked up the courage to do the same for Rosalind.'

'She does not care for me.' Richard shut his eyes for a moment and drew a deep breath. 'And even if she did, how could I ask her to marry someone like myself? She deserves better. She deserves a younger man, one without the kind of reputation I have been at such pains to acquire – and which now is like dust and ashes to me.'

'She may deserve better,' Julian admitted. 'I am sure Cassandra deserves a better man than I am. But she loves me. Perhaps Rosalind has feelings for you as well. Come, man! Did she never give you any sign?'

'I kissed her once,' St George muttered reluctantly. 'That night when we walked together in the abbey garden.'

Julian blinked. 'You never mentioned this to me before.'

'I – I could not.'

'She was not . . . repulsed by your advances?'

'No.'

Julian considered his friend's bent head, as if he bore the weight of the world on those broad shoulders. He was being consumed by his own love for a woman, which must undoubtedly be a novel sensation to him.

'Go back to her, Richard,' he said softly. 'Tell her how you feel.'

'But what if she should reject me?' He looked up and Julian was shocked yet again at the fear and pain in those clear hazel eyes. 'I could not bear it if she did so. I could not.'

'I have never seen a man so deep in love – nor one so stubborn!' Julian said to his uncle later that evening.

'I guessed as much,' Sir Jasper said, seeming mighty pleased with himself.

'Since you know so much, perhaps you can tell me if Miss Powell is in love with him as well?'

He tapped a finger against his chin. 'I should say that it is very likely. If you want to be certain, of course, you must ask Miss Cassandra. She is her cousin's confidante, I'm sure.'

'Yes, of course.' Julian brightened. 'But I doubt if St George would believe me if I told him so.'

'He might think you told him only to push him into proposing to her,' his uncle conceded.

'His damned pride!'

'How right it is that "an haughty spirit goeth before a fall".'

'St George has certainly fallen. But if what we suspect is true, Miss Powell must also be very unhappy.'

'Probably.'

'You do not seem very concerned about either of them,' Julian said sourly.

'Should I be?'

'Well, I cannot sit idly by while they are both nursing wounded hearts. I must *do* something.'

'Far be it from me to interfere in the lives of others,' Sir

Jasper said magniloquently. 'It generally does nothing but harm to become involved in such matters. But if you will be advised by me, my boy, I think I may be able to devise a little deception which might prove efficacious.'

'What do you mean, sir?'

'It will take courage and daring, mind you.'

'Whatever it takes, it must be done!'

INTERLUDE

Lady Bettisham, the very same person who has already been mentioned as the mother of the unfortunate Richard St George, emerged from her bedchamber at eleven o'clock in the morning. It was several days since the meeting between her son and Julian – a meeting of which she was, of course, completely ignorant.

She had awakened over an hour before, but her *toilette* was laborious and she never felt in any condition to present herself to her acquaintance without first undergoing a rigorous regimen of ablutions and the application of an artfully arranged mask which produced just the effect which she desired.

Settling herself gracefully upon a sofa, she rang for some lukewarm tea and a wafer-thin piece of toast. One could not keep a girlish figure at her age without drastically reducing one's consumption of meals, after all.

The maid delivered the requested sustenance, curtsied and made her exit. Along with this dessicated breakfast was a copy of the day's *Gazette*, which milady languidly perused for several minutes before her eye caught a paragraph of particular interest.

She stiffened at once, crushing the paper in her claw-like hand. In fact, the under-housemaid, passing by at that moment, was arrested in her progress by one glance at her apparently paralytic employer. Upon closer inspection, the poor maid wished that she had had the presence of mind to run swiftly past the portal, for it was now clear to her that Lady B. was not paralysed. In fact, she was in that state of mind peculiar to the idle rich when they are confronted by an unpleasant dilemma: undetermined whether it were best to swoon or slap the nearest servant.

'Girl!' Lady Bettisham screeched, not bothering to ring for anyone, since succour appeared to be already at hand. 'Go,' she continued in that strident voice. 'Go and tell Brodman to make my carriage ready – at once!'

At the very moment when she was clamouring for transportation, her son was picking up a copy of the *Gazette* for himself. He did not generally pay much attention to it, but some anonymous friend had left a copy at his door with a note to the effect that he might read something of interest to himself therein.

For some time he searched its pages, trying vainly to determine what there could possibly be that pertained to him. He was almost about to discard the blasted thing when the words he sought leapt out at him from amongst the jumble of print. For a moment he stared down at it, quite as shocked as his poor mama had been. Then, as if by magic, the languor which had engulfed him these past weeks fell from him like an old coat. He rose up from his chair, sober and resolved upon immediate action.

'Brenton!' He called for his man, who appeared but seconds after. 'Ah! There you are.'

'What is it, sir?' Brenton asked, puzzled by this sudden burst of activity.

'I need to shave,' St George announced. 'Also, draw me a

191

bath and lay out clean driving attire.'

'Yes, sir!' Brenton struggled to keep up with his master, who was advancing through the house at great speed, talking all the time.

'Oh, and have the groom see that the greys are harnessed. I will be driving the phaeton today.'

Brenton stared at him in blank astonishment. The change in him was so sudden and so complete. The man he had known and admired all these years had all but disappeared in these past weeks, but now he had miraculously returned. What had happened?

'Don't stand there gawking, man!' St George commanded. 'I must be ready within the hour. Be quick about it. Go now!'

It was another day before the inhabitants of rural Buckinghamshire received their copies of the *Gazette*. The news it bore might be a day old, but its effect was just as profound as it had been in London.

At the hunting lodge, Sir Jasper read the interesting item and handed it silently to Julian. He looked at it, raised his brows and passed it on to Mrs Plummer. Her reaction was much less muted than that of the two men.

'Goodness gracious!' she cried. 'Bless my soul! I cannot eye my beliefs! Can this be true?'

'It says so in plain English,' Julian pointed out unnecessarily.

'But I have heard nothing of this.' She placed a plump hand against an equally plump cheek in wonderment. 'Not but what it is a fine thing if it were true.'

'There is only one way to be sure,' Sir Jasper suggested.

'I shall get the landau ready,' Julian said. 'Shall we all go?'

The moving piece of prose which set so many people rushing

for their conveyances was received at the abbey with equal surprise, though it did not produce a demand for horses nor a general exodus.

It was Mr Woodford who made the discovery as he sat with Cassandra and Rosalind at breakfast. The two women were talking – as women are wont to do – about the wedding. They paid little heed to the *Gazette* until the gentleman drew their attention to it.

'I think you should see this, Rosalind,' he remarked, frowning.

'What is it, Uncle?'

'Utter nonsense, I should say.' Mr Woodford proceeded to deliver a brief lecture on the sad decline in modern journalism. 'Such a smattering of half-truths and downright lies, couched in the most execrable language! How one misses Dr Johnson.'

While he was absorbed in his own effusiveness, Rosalind had time actually to read the offending notice. She blinked. She grew hot, then cold. She shook her head in bewilderment, then read the words once more. After reading it for the third time, she was convinced that it was not, after all, an illusion.

'How can this be?' she wondered aloud. 'Who could have – how could they have made such a mistake?'

'They must issue an apology,' Mr Woodford said. 'I will write them a letter this very day.'

'What is it? What is wrong?' Cassandra asked, quite put out by this mysterious message which had so upset everyone.

'I still cannot believe it.'

'But what does it *say*?'

'It says—'

CHAPTER TWENTY-ONE

'Someone is coming.' Cassandra tilted her head to one side, listening.

Rosalind had heard the noise too. It was a quiet morning, and visitors were still few at the abbey, so the sound of an approaching carriage was enough to halt Rosalind in the middle of her explanation. Her voice trailed off. Julian usually arrived on horseback, unless he brought Mrs Plummer or his uncle with him. She had scarcely enough time to consider this conjecture when voices in the hall indicated that those very same persons had indeed arrived.

'Miss Powell!' Cousin Priscilla exclaimed, bustling forward. 'Such happy news! Why did you not tell us? So creditive as you have been . . . I cannot secret it.'

Trying to disentangle the ravelled skein of her words, Rosalind soon realized that she spoke of the announcement she had just read. Oh dear! Did everyone know of it? Seeing the smiles and the look of expectancy on the faces of the two gentlemen behind her, however, she needed no further affirmation that they, at least, were conversant with the situation.

'I assure you that I knew nothing of this, ma'am,' Rosalind said vehemently. 'I cannot imagine who could have perpetrated such a dreaful hoax—'

Once more her explanations were interrupted by the sound of an approaching carriage. In this instance, it seemed to be driven by a regular Jehu, for the clatter of hooves was pronounced and the gravel being churned up might have been the result of a whirlwind.

'Who can that be?' Cassandra exclaimed. Nobody else was likely to be paying a call at the abbey. Indeed, they had no other acquaintance in the country to visit them.

'Someone in a great hurry, it seems.'

Sir Jasper, who made this comment, exchanged a speaking glance with Julian which made Rosalind eye them both with suspicion. Something they knew which she did not. What kind of game was Julian's uncle playing now?

They were all still as statues, anticipating the entrance of the next player in their little comedy. Nor did they have long to wait. It was mere seconds later when a loud pounding assaulted their ears. Someone was seeking admittance, and would obviously not be denied. Debenham must have opened the front door pretty quickly, for they soon heard a loud stomping advancing towards them at a rapid pace, and Debenham's voice calling out to the stomper, asking him whither he was going and whether he thought this house was his own residence.

'I do not need you to announce me!' the person he addressed called back to him, his voice loud and strong. 'Go about your business, my man.'

Hearing that voice, Rosalind wondered at the contrariness of her own heart. Even as it rose into her throat, it quailed at the thought of the coming confrontation. If only she could run away! If only she might disappear behind the green satin curtains at the narrow gothic windows, like a spectre flitting through the walls. Instead, she stood with her feet planted firmly on the ground, knowing that she was about to face both her greatest joy and greatest fear.

Standing in the doorway, a crumpled issue of the *Gazette* in his clenched left hand, was Richard St George. He was plainly livid, and magnificent (at least to one person there) in his wrath. He greeted no one, and the assembled company was suspended in anticipation and failed to remark upon it – or to offer their own greetings.

'Are you responsible for this, ma'am?' His gaze was fastened upon Rosalind as he held out the offending document. 'Is this your doing?'

With the exception of Cassandra, who was truly 'in the dark', all eyes now focused upon Rosalind. She did not notice them, however, and was therefore spared any self-consciousness which she might have felt. It is wonderful how efficacious total rage can be in times of distress.

'I?' She flung the word at him like a gauntlet. Battle was now fairly joined. 'What reason could I possibly have to play such a foolish trick?'

'What, in heaven's name, is happening? What are you all talking about?' Cassandra wailed, almost beside herself with frustrated curiosity.

'You might, perhaps, have thought to trap me into marriage,' St George replied, ignoring her plea. The fire in his eyes died down to a dim glow and he seemed more hesitant.

'Marry you?' Rosalind actually took a step forward, her fury building to a crescendo worthy of Signor Rossini at his loudest. 'I would scorn to ally myself to the likes of you, sir! The very thought is disgusting to me.'

The gentleman thus addressed caught his lips between his teeth. Whatever he might have said to this would never be known, for at that moment they were interrupted by the arrival of the final member of their cast. For the third time that morning, the sound of carriage wheels was heard upon the front drive.

'Who is it now?' Cassandra demanded of nobody in particular.

'A person of great interest, I'll wager,' Sir Jasper answered her, while Julian went to her side and began to whisper in her ear.

Whoever it might be, Rosalind no longer cared very much. Her emotions were in such turmoil that, whether it were the Archbishop of Canterbury or Satan himself, she would have met either of them with equal temerity. In fact, it was neither of these august personages. The latest addition to their happy band, who entered the room but a minute or two later, was a woman – one somewhat advanced in years but very well preserved. She was clearly a person of quality, and one whom Rosalind had never seen before in her life. A panting Debenham stood behind her. It seemed he was fated to be denied the opportunity of announcing anyone today. In the end, it was quite unnecessary, for St George revealed her identity with one simple word:

'Mama!'

'Lady Bettisham!' Mrs Plummer exclaimed, displaying her usual cheerful smile. 'How good it is to see you again. It has been a long time.'

Lady Bettisham looked the lady up and down, taking in her usual piebald appearance, and not even the most generous onlooker could describe her appraisal as in the least encouraging. 'I cannot recall having ever met you before, madam,' she answered with icy disdain.

'No.' Mrs Plummer stepped back a pace. 'Now that I think

on it, you never could.'

'That was not well done, indeed, Mother.' St George was clearly not pleased. 'That lady is our cousin, Mrs Plummer.'

'It is not a connection which I care to acknowledge.'

'If I were you, ma'am,' Rosalind said, addressing Cousin Priscilla, 'I would not mind such ill-bred persons. You clearly lose nothing by severing any connection with such a disagreeable relation.'

Lady Bettisham reddened alarmingly at this description of herself. Before she could respond in kind, however, her son forestalled her.

'What are you doing here, Mama?'

'I have come,' she declared, stiffening her back as though prepared for resistance, 'to save you from contracting what is clearly a terrible *mésalliance*. Who,' she continued, 'is this "Miss Rosalind Powell" to whom the notice in the *Gazette* claims that you are betrothed?'

'I am Miss Powell,' Rosalind answered for him.

Lady Bettisham turned to face her, treating her to much the same inspection as she had just inflicted upon Mrs Plummer. But this time the object of her scorn gave her back look for look without flinching, in a manner to which the peeress was plainly not accustomed. She returned her gaze to her son, therefore, directing her remarks to him.

'This woman is clearly an adventuress, who has used her undeniable beauty to entrap you, my poor boy.' She paused for a moment, perhaps diverted by a hastily stifled giggle from Cassandra. 'But have you no thought for your family name? Have you no consideration for duty and honour? I could not believe it when I went to your lodgings, only to learn that you had run off to be with this woman. If you marry her, you are no longer my son!'

'I would advise you to say no more, ma'am.' St George's brow darkened, his lips growing pinched and white as he listened to his mother's speech. 'Kindly remember that you are speaking of the woman I love.'

'You have taken leave of your senses,' Lady Bettisham cried.

'If I have, it is no concern of yours.'

'Of course it is my concern. I am your mother – your own flesh and blood.'

While they were speaking, Rosalind moved from her spot in the centre of the room and came to stand beside St George, so that they stood together, facing his mother.

'It is a pity,' she said to the older woman, 'that you did not remember that fact before, ma'am.'

'I have nothing to say to this person.' Lady Bettisham averted her gaze from the couple before her.

'But I have a great deal to say to you, Lady Bettisham,' Rosalind replied. 'You may not care to look at me, but you shall hear me this day.'

'How dare you address me in such a fashion?' The other woman twisted her neck about again, to fix hard blue eyes upon the girl she had chosen to despise.

'I know something of your character, madam.' Rosalind's bosom heaved in her righteous wrath. 'Sir Jasper has informed us that you were well aware of your son's purpose in coming into Buckinghamshire – that he intended my seduction. Nor had you any qualms about it. Oh no! You found it quite amusing, I believe.'

Lady Bettisham shrugged carelessly, in a manner much like her son. 'Young girls must take their chances. If they are foolish, that is not my affair.'

'A rake must also take his chances,' Rosalind shot back. 'You cared nothing that the lives of two innocent young women might be ruined, but now that the tables have turned, you are all concern. If I have ensnared your son, you have no cause to object to it. To the victor the spoils.'

'You impudent strumpet!' The lady's anger could not be disguised. 'Will you allow her to speak to me in this insolent manner, St George?'

'She would not have done so,' her son reminded her harshly, 'had you not chosen to interfere in my affairs, and to insult this lady in the most intolerable fashion.'

'Your son would have been better had he been born to a she-wolf, rather than to such a woman as you,' Rosalind said, warming to her theme. 'You never cared for his welfare, never gave him the affection which every child deserves from its mother. But now that you fear his actions may stain your precious family name, you thrust yourself into his life with no other intention than to separate him from someone who loves him far more than you have ever done!'

This impassioned discourse seemed to rob Lady Bettisham of breath, for she was silent for some seconds afterward. This gave her son time to digest the last words which Rosalind had spoken, at which point he seized her by the shoulders and spun her around to face him.

'Is it true?' he demanded. 'Do you love me, Rosalind?'

'Yes,' she said simply, having gone too far now to deny it.

'Thank God!' he cried, and before the assembled company he completely abandoned any pretence at decorum, drawing Rosalind fully into his embrace and pressing a passionate kiss upon her upturned lips.

'St George!' his mother cried, scandalized.

Rosalind, meanwhile, had completely forgotten her adversary and everyone else in the room. She was lost in the inexpressible joy of feeling his arms about her once more and savouring the wonder of his kiss. When at last he raised his head, it was to her alone that he spoke.

'My dearest dragon,' he said huskily, 'how can you possibly love me, knowing all that you do of me?'

'How can I help but love you?' she asked, lifting a hand to stroke his cheek. 'I have never seen a man who so needed to be loved.'

'And I have never known a woman who had such love to give,' he whispered. 'I love you with all my heart. I cannot conceive what I have ever done to deserve you, but if you will do me the honour of becoming my wife, I shall be the happiest and proudest man in England.'

'But I do not believe in spotless leopards, nor in reformed rakes,' she quizzed him.

'Marry me,' he urged, 'and I will make a believer of you yet, my little doubter.'

'Are you quite certain that you wish to marry me?'

'I have never been so certain of anything in my life. Besides,' he added wickedly, 'we are officially betrothed. It says so in the *Gazette*. So you cannot cry off now, my love. Despite the repugnance which you very properly expressed but a few minutes ago, you *must* marry me.'

'Very well, then. I will.'

He would have kissed her again, but his mother interrupted this tender scene with words which were anything but romantic.

'I absolutely forbid such a union!'

'Mother,' he said, 'keep your breath to cool your coffee. If anyone here is contracting a *mésalliance*, it is Miss Powell. I am certain that she could do much better than to marry me.'

'She is a penniless nobody,' Lady Bettisham argued.

'Not penniless, ma'am,' Mr Woodford interjected at this

point in the proceedings. 'I have long determined that, should Rosalind marry, I would settle a sum of six thousand pounds upon her as a dowry.'

'You see how wrong you are, Mama?' St George smiled, looking more youthful and at ease than any there had ever seen him. 'I am marrying an heiress. And as to her being a nobody, never have you been so mistaken.'

'I see,' Lady Bettisham said at last, 'that you will not listen to reason. If you are determined upon this dreadful course, there is no more to be said. But do not think that you will ever again be received at my house – or that of any other of your family.'

'That,' he replied drily, 'will not be so very different from my present situation.'

'I had hoped,' she said with great dignity, 'that at least you would remember what you owe to your own mother.'

'I do not forget,' he said. 'But I believe that the Scriptures tell us that when a man marries he leaves his father and mother and cleaves to his wife. I intend to cleave to mine as few men have ever cleaved before.'

'Very well then,' she answered. 'I wash my hands of you.'

At this point in the proceedings, a diversion was created by a most unlikely source. Unnoticed by anyone, a certain mischievous feline lay in wait beneath one of the chairs nearby. Lady Bettisham's gown sported a satin sash with a rich tassle at the end, hanging down the side almost to the floor. As she moved and spoke, it dangled enticingly until the poor kitten could resist no longer. Without warning, it suddenly sprang from beneath the chair and dashed up the length of the sash until it was just beneath the lady's waist.

All eyes in the room were turned towards this fantastic denouement, the lady staring down in horrified surprise at the bundle of grey fur and claws which swung from her own gown.

At the same moment, Welly, attracted by his feline friend's antics, darted from behind the sofa, bulging black eyes staring up at Lady Bettisham, barking furiously.

In a flash, St George reached out and snatched the kitten from his mother's outraged person. Julian scooped up the noisy pug.

'Mama,' her unrepentant prodigal said, struggling to contain his mirth, 'allow me to introduce you to the Duchess of Folbrook Abbey!'

The entire company then fell into whoops, which quite confounded the poor lady. She glared at them harder then ever.

'This is clearly a madhouse!' she cried, adding, 'I wish you well, St George. When you have come to your senses, you will see how foolish you have been.'

'Lady Bettisham,' Rosalind said to her, more calmly than she had yet spoken, 'I have no desire to wound the woman who is soon to become my mother-in-law, but I would advise you to consider carefully before you turn your back on your only son because of me. I will be his wife and the mother of his children – and your grandchildren. Though I may not be welcome at your house, you will always be welcome at ours – should you choose to enter it.'

She might have spoken to stone, for all the effect her words had. Lady Bettisham glanced around at all of them before sweeping out of the room in a decided dudgeon. It was not long before they heard her carriage driving away.

'I think we had best be going,' Sir Jasper said, upon her departure. 'It has been a most enjoyable morning, but time has slipped away from us and I think these young people have much to discuss without our presence.'

Amidst much incomprehensible murmurings from Cousin

Priscilla, he made haste to leave, while Julian protested that he would stay rather longer. St George promised to drive him back to the lodge, and the others at last took their leave.

'I hope you will forgive me for my words to your mother,' Rosalind said to her betrothed.

'What did you say that she did not deserve?' he countered. 'I have never been close to her, and frankly it is much more difficult for me to forgive her for her refusal to see *your* worth.'

'I find it hard to forgive that she could not see yours.'

'I do not know that anyone but you has ever seen that, my beloved dragon.'

'If only you were not so determined to hide it from the world!' she said, as he raised her hand to his lips. 'But despite all that your family and that London could do to sophisticate you into insensibility, your heart remains true.'

'My heart was a most indifferent organ, until I met you,' Richard said simply. 'I have discovered that a heart is worth nothing until you give it to someone.'

'But if neither of you placed the notice of your wedding in the *Gazette*,' Cassandra asked them, reverting to a subject now all but forgotten, 'then who is responsible?'

Julian gave a slight cough. 'I'm afraid it was my doing.'

'You!' the other four sang out in unison.

'I knew you were both in love with each other,' he defended himself. 'But it seemed that neither of you would ever admit to it, nor were you likely to see each other again if something were not done.'

'It was undoubtedly a masterly plan,' St George admitted. 'I shall be eternally grateful to you, my friend.'

'If you must express your gratitude, let it be to my uncle.'

'Sir Jasper?' Rosalind asked, surprised.

'His was the mind which conceived the plan. I merely executed it.'

'It seems that, one way or another, Sir Jasper has been instrumental in bringing all of us together.'

'Indeed, we must be grateful to him,' Julian agreed, looking down tenderly at Cassandra.

'But I have just realized,' St George exclaimed to Mr Woodford, 'that I have not actually approached you to offer for Rosalind, sir,'

'I think,' the older man said, 'that we may dispense with such formalities. How could I withhold my consent now?'

'Your consent is not even needed, Papa,' Cassandra reminded him. 'Rosalind is no schoolgirl, after all.'

'It seems,' Mr Woodford quipped, 'that, despite your best efforts, St George, the dragon has defeated you.'

'Say rather, that love has defeated us both,' Rosalind corrected him.

'In this case, defeat is so much sweeter than victory,' her love added. 'My only regret is that I do not have a Special Licence, so that we may be married along with Cassandra and Julian three days hence.'

Another cough from Julian, who reached into the lining of his coat and pulled out a sheaf of paper.

'Consider this,' he said, 'in the nature of a wedding present.'

It was, of course, the very document which they sought. A double wedding was inevitable, it seemed.

'But I hate to leave you alone here at the abbey, Papa,' Cassandra said, with sudden contrition.

'Doubtless, Mr Woodford will soon have his grandchildren and his niece's children to occupy his time,' St George commented, enjoying the rush of colour in Rosalind's cheeks.

'Perhaps you will marry again,' Cassandra said, brightening at the thought. In a moment of pure mischief, she added, 'Mrs Plummer is of a pleasant disposition.'

Mr Woodford shook his head in a decided negative.

'I can assure you,' he said, 'I shall not be *that* lonely!'